THE KINGFISH.

Stories from

Around

the World

KINGFISHER
a Houghton Mifflin Company imprint
222 Berkeley Street
Boston, Massachusetts 02116
www.houghtonmifflinbooks.com

First published in 1993
2 4 6 8 10 9 7 5 3 1
1TR/0404/THOM/MA/115IWF(F)

LIBRARY OF CONGRESS CATALOGING-IN-PUBLICATION DATA
Stories from around the world/illustrated by Victor Ambrus:
chosen by Linda Jennings.—1st American ed.
p. cm.
Summary: A collection of 17 traditional tales from such parts
of the world as Africa, Japan, and South America.
1. Tales. [1. Folklore] I. Jennings, Linda. M. II. Ambrus, Victor G., ill.
PZ8.I.T696 1993 398.2—dc20 [E] 92–43153 CIP AC

ISBN 0-7534-5727-X

Printed in India

THE KINGFISHER TREASURY OF

Stories from Around the World

CHOSEN BY LINDA JENNINGS

ILLUSTRATED BY VICTOR AMBRUS

KINGFISHER

BOSTON

CONTENTS

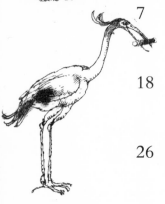

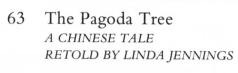

The publisher would like to thank the copyright holders for permission to reproduce the following copyright material:

THE GIANT'S DAUGHTER

*A Scandinavian tale
retold by Ethel Johnston-Phelps*

A long time ago, giants and trolls dwelt in the high mountain forests above the northern fjords. They kept to themselves and had little to do with the people who lived in the valley below – except to scare the wits out of one of them now and then.

Gina was different; she was quite curious about the humans living in the little houses down in the valley and along the shore. Of course, she was still young, as giants go, and not fully grown. That would explain her foolishness, thought her father.

"She has the curiosity of a bear cub," grumbled her mother, "but it's very unnatural to bother with humankind."

"Have nothing to do with people," advised the elder giants. "Small, stupid creatures! Frightened

7

by a boulder thrown or a sheep carried off!"

Nonetheless, on clear days, young Gina would sit on a rock at the lower edge of the forest, watching the people below go about their daily work. It seemed to Gina that these people had a splendid time; the maidservants especially caught her attention, moving about from dairy to stream, laughing together as they worked.

"The work is so easy, I could do it with one hand," thought she. "And so many kinds of food just for the taking!" Gina, it must be admitted, was just a little greedy. She loved to eat.

She was also quite stubborn. Once she had made up her mind to go down to the village below, no one could dissuade her.

Her cousins, the mountain trolls, shrilled, "But they are our enemy! You will be killed, and it will serve you right."

"You foolish child," cried her mother in alarm. "Mark my words, there will be trouble. No good will come of it."

"No good will come of it!" warned the uncles, the aunts, and all the rest of the giants.

But they were all quite wrong.

One day Gina, hop-skipping over the boulders, came down the mountain to the village. At the first two houses where she stopped to ask for work, she had no luck at all.

At the third house, the mistress looked at the very tall, strongly-built girl with the large round head and thought, "Here's a bargain indeed! An odd-looking country girl, but she'll do very well for chopping wood and pounding the wash." She told Gina to come in.

Gina bent down, ducking her head to enter the house. "Such queer, tiny houses," thought she. "Doorways much too small, roofs much too low for comfort."

Gina was set to work at once, but it was not many days before the mistress regretted having taken in the strange girl. Gina chopped wood with a will, but so violently that the chunks flew in all directions – one struck a rooster stone dead; one sent a dog yowling off in surprise; another whacked a cart horse so sharply that he bolted off, spilling rounds of cheese right and left. Then she carried such huge armloads of wood into the house that the door burst off its hinges.

Set to work with a tub of wash at the stream, she pounded the laundry so thoroughly that all the clothes and linens came out in rags.

To make matters worse, Gina ate more than all the other servants put together. Even between meals, she found her way into the storeroom and sat happily devouring jars of honey, vats of pickles, and long strings of sausages.

The mistress brought this tale of woe to her husband, a merchant. "She is impossible!" cried the mistress. "We must get rid of her. When she scours pots, she grinds holes in them! When she washes dishes, she breaks half of them! If she sits on my chairs, they collapse. No, I can't keep her a day longer; she'll be the ruin of us!"

But if Gina was greedy for food, the merchant was miserly about money. "She's powerfully strong, and we pay her no wages," he pointed out to his wife – for Gina knew nothing of money or wages. "We could never get a village girl to work for us without payment. And where could we find one half so strong? Gina's twice as strong as a man. I'll find work for her."

So, although the mistress complained bitterly about the havoc Gina caused and wanted to get rid of her at once, the merchant insisted she be kept on.

He set Gina to heavy outdoor work, carrying bales of hay to the barn. But Gina thought it fun to toss the bales into the hayloft, and if she knocked down a farmhand in the process, she merely roared with laughter. If a horse kicked her, she gave the animal a powerful kick right back. All this caused such an uproar in the barnyard that the merchant quickly set Gina to unloading the fishing boats that came to his wharf. Here she did the work of two or three men.

Delighted with such a strong and willing worker, the merchant used Gina everywhere – from sausage and cheese making to building a new storage barn. In the new barn, he had Gina build a room and bed of her own, for the mistress declared that she was not fit to live in a house. The merchant, however, rubbed his hands in satisfaction thinking of the money he saved.

And what about Gina? Gina was enjoying herself. The heavy work did not bother her at all. She joined in the village dances, but she swung her partners with such vigor that they whirled away across the field. After that, partners were hard to find. Still, everything new fascinated her. Although she thought humans most peculiar in their ways, she marveled at their cleverness.

Their houses were too small, their furniture too flimsy, but it was fine to sleep on a bed instead of a pile of leaves, or use an ax to chop wood instead of breaking it apart with her hands. And to think one might keep chickens to have eggs whenever one wished! Her sharp, inquisitive eyes took in everything that went on around her.

Things went on in this way for several months. But while the merchant became more and more pleased with his bargain, the mistress became more and more irritated with Gina. She determined to get rid of her.

In the spring, the merchant prepared to sail down to Bergen on a trading voyage. His wife announced that she would go with him. Just before they set sail, she took Gina aside and said sharply, "I don't want to find you here when we return. I advise you to go back to wherever you came from!"

Then she quickly joined her husband aboard the ship, and they sailed away down the fjord on a stiff breeze.

Gina was left on shore with the village folk who had turned out to see the merchant off. Next to her stood two maidservants from the village.

"Wish you were going with them?" said one. "Save the money they pay you, Gina, and you can go to Bergen yourself someday!"

"Money they pay me?" repeated Gina in surprise.

"Your wages for working," said the other. "I noticed you never spend any money. You must have a nice little sum hidden away!"

"They never gave me any money for working!"

The two girls laughed at her. "Oh, you *are* a green one! You worked almost a year for nothing?"

"Greedy old man," said the other. "No wonder he's so rich!"

When Gina finally understood that all the other country girls were paid, her eyes became quite red with anger. She stalked back to the merchant's place. There she sat down and thought for a long time.

"Payment I shall have,"
she said finally. "I'll take it myself!"
At once, she set to work. She pulled out an old cart from the barn and loaded it with all the things she had decided to take with her. In went a rooster and a hen, an ax, nails – she knew what she needed for the success of her plan. And when the cart was filled, she didn't forget to toss in a round wheel of cheese, a crock of pickles, and several strings of her favorite sausages.

Then she pulled the loaded cart up the mountain until she reached the high pine forests, the land of the trolls and giants.

Swinging the ax with gusto, she soon converted trees into the framework of a tall one-room

15

house. She made sure that the doorway was big and wide, and the roof high enough for a full-grown giant. Next to it was a fenced-in run for the rooster and hen.

From time to time, the giants and trolls came by to watch her work and to gape in astonishment at so much mad activity.

"Poor Gina," they said to each other. "She's become as crazy as a loon, living with humans all that time. I knew no good would come of it!"

"She'll never marry now," lamented Gina's mother. "She's collected no fur pelts for her dowry. What sensible giant would want that pile of wood?"

But again they were all quite wrong.

When Gina had finished all her work, the first frost sparkled on the ground, and the smell of snow was in the air. She now had a tall house made of logs, snug against the winter cold. She had an open hearth and a stack of firewood; a big, solid chair; a large bed covered with fur pelts; chickens safely housed in a lean-to; rounds of cheese made from wild goat and reindeer milk; sausages and wild boar hams hanging from the rafters.

By the time the heavy snow had settled on the mountain, even the sour trolls had to admit that the warm log house was better than a cave or a deep underground hole. It dawned on the folk of the forest that Gina was not crazy at all. She was in fact very clever.

And what better dowry could a young giant girl have than a snug hut and strings of fragrant sausages? All the giant folk now called her Clever Gina, and as the winter thawed into spring, Gina was besieged with offers to marry.

"Perhaps I'll marry, or perhaps I won't," she said carelessly. "I'll think about it." And since the young giants were very eager to bring her rabbits or wild boar in exchange for eggs, cheese, or the loan of her ax, it seemed to Gina that "thinking about it" was a very good arrangement indeed.

THE GREAT GREEDY BEAST

An African tale
retold by Amabel Williams-Ellis

L ong, long ago, there were some people who
lived in a nice valley among the mountains;
this was in Africa. The only way to get to the
village where they lived was through a narrow
place – what they called a *nek*. The mountains
round about were so high and steep that you
couldn't get into the valley any other way, and
the nek really was very narrow.

One day, a Great Greedy Beast was feeling very
hungry. He crawled and he crawled until he came
to the nek, and he put his nose down and he
snuffed, and he could smell people and cattle, and
hens, and all sorts of live things.

Well, he hadn't had any food for quite a long
time, and he was hungry and he wasn't fat any
more, wasn't that Great Greedy Beast. He tried
to follow that delicious smell, and he tried to get
through the narrow nek in the mountains. For a

long time he couldn't, but at last he got so thin that he just managed to squeeze through. Then the dreadful creature ate everything he could find in that village!

He ate all the people, did that Great Greedy Beast. He ate all the dogs, all the cows, and all the hens. At least he *thought* he had eaten every living thing and everybody!

But there was a woman with a new baby who had seen him coming – just this one woman – and he hadn't smelled her. This was because, as soon as she spied him, she had smeared herself all over with the ashes from the dust heap, and she had smeared her baby all over with the same dust.

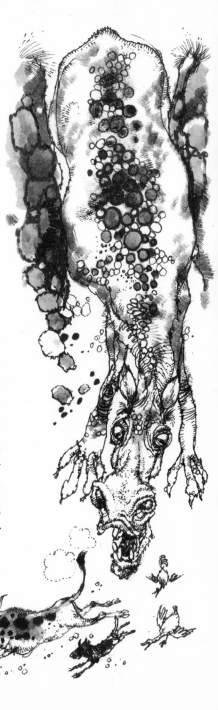

Then she had gone out of her hut where she lived, and she had crept into a little hut where they generally kept the calves.

When the Great Greedy Beast had finished eating all the people and all the cattle and all the goats, and all the dogs and all the hens, he went around to see if he had left anything. He put his snout close to the little hut where the woman and her baby were hiding, and he snuffed! And then he snuffed again! But all he could smell was gone-away calves and ashes, so he too went away.

Away he crawled. He crawled and he crawled till he came to the nek in the mountains.

He had once been thin and hungry, but now this Great Greedy Beast had eaten such a lot that he was fat and all swelled out. He was so fat now that, try as he would, he couldn't get through, and so, of course, he had to stay where he was.

That Great Greedy Beast didn't bother about this. He thought that not being able to get out

20

didn't matter that much! He felt sure that he had eaten everything there was to eat, so there was no one left to attack him, so he could just lie there and go to sleep. So that was what he did. He just shut his eyes and slept.

But as soon as the Great Greedy Beast had crawled out of the village and off to the nek, the woman opened the door of the little hut. Then she dusted off the ashes she had rubbed on herself, and she dusted her baby as well. All those ashes had made her thirsty, and she thought she had better go and get some water. Also she wanted to make sure that the Great Greedy Beast hadn't drunk all the water in the river, as well as eating all the people and animals. So she set down her baby in the hut, and off she went down to the river and had a drink.

But when she came back, instead of her baby, she found a grown man – a splendid warrior – sitting there in the little hut that was used for calves.

He was a splendid man, this warrior, armed with spears and bush knives and with a huge shield.

"Man!" said she in fright. "What have you done with my baby?"

"Mother," said he in his deep man's voice, "I *am* your baby."

"But you were only born the day before yesterday!" said she.

"Never mind about that," said he. "What has happened? Where have all the people gone?"

At this his mother began to sob. "Oh," said she, "the people have all been eaten by the Great Greedy Beast, as well as all the cattle, the dogs, the sheep and the goats, and the hens."

"That must be a terrible sort of monster!" said he.

"Yes, he is that!" said she. "But I managed to hide you from him all the same."

"Well, where is the Great Greedy Beast?"

"Come out and let us see, my child," said she.

So the woman and the splendid warrior, with his spears and his leopard-skin belt with his big knives with antelope-horn handles stuck in it, climbed onto the roof of the calves' hut. Then his mother pointed up to the nek, which was the only way of getting to their valley, and she said, "Son, do you see that thing with a head that nearly fills up the nek? Well, that thing really isn't part of the mountain, *that* is the Great Greedy Beast!"

"Well," said he, "we'll soon see to that!" And he began to climb down off the roof of the hut.

He had three spears with him, and a shield and those big knives as well. Off he strode! And his mother followed him and called out to him, "But, Son, you were only born the day before

yesterday! You're not going to try and fight that terrible monster?"

"Oh yes, I am," said he. "You'll see, Mother dear. It'll be all right!"

Well, as you can guess, his mother couldn't stop him! So off he went. He walked with long strides to the nek where the monster lay. But he stopped twice on the way. Why? To sharpen his spears and his knives on flat stones.

When he got near, the monster smelled him, and when it smelled him, it opened one eye, and then it opened its huge mouth to try to swallow him.

But you see, it was stuck! It couldn't turn! It had eaten so much that it couldn't get up, so when it opened that huge mouth, the warrior just skipped aside and got behind the monster's jaws. Then, with all his might, he stabbed it once, twice and thrice in the back of the neck, once with each of his three spears, and at the third spear–stab, it died.

23

Next the warrior took one of the big knives with antelope-horn handles that he had in his belt, and he began to cut. Soon, from inside the animal, a man's voice said, "Oh, don't cut me! Don't cut me!"

So he left off cutting in that place and began to cut again, lower down. But now came another voice from inside, and this one said, "Moo-moo." (That, as you can guess, was one of the cows that the Great Greedy Beast had swallowed.) Once more, the warrior stopped cutting and began at a third place.

This time, from inside the Great Greedy Beast, he heard a different sound, a "Kwee! Kwee! Kwee!" (That was a shrill dog's bark, as you can guess.)

So for a fourth time he began cutting at yet

another new place. "Cock-o-cock-a-loo! Cock-o-cock-a-loo!" (You can guess what that was.)

But this time the warrior shouted out, "I'm sick and tired of cutting in new places! You're only a rooster, just you get out of the way yourself!" So the rooster moved over and the warrior went on cutting, and he cut until he opened a big door in the side of the Great Greedy Beast.

Then, when it was open, all the people and the children, and the sheep, goats, cattle, and all the dogs and cats and chickens came out, all of them alive and well!

The end of it was that they made the warrior and his mother the chieftains of the village, and all the people and the children feasted and danced and drummed and shouted for joy because they had been saved from the Great Greedy Beast.

RICKY OF
THE TUFT

A French fairy tale
retold by Linda Jennings

When a queen gives birth to her first child, it is usually a time of great happiness and rejoicing. Once, however, there was a queen who found no such happiness when she looked down at her baby son. He was extremely ugly — there was no doubt about that — and he had a ridiculous little tuft of hair that grew straight up from the top of his head. Because of this, he was known as Ricky of the Tuft.

"Why have I been burdened with such a hideous child," cried the queen. "No princess will look at him when he is old enough to marry."

Now Ricky of the Tuft had a fairy godmother, as was usual in those days for the children of kings and queens. This godmother looked long and hard at the ugly little baby, and sighed deeply.

"I cannot make him handsome," she said. "But I can make him clever, sensible, and kind. And when he grows up, he will be able to bestow this gift of cleverness and good sense upon the person he loves best."

The queen had to be content with this, although she was not happy about it. Oh, why could her son not be both clever *and* handsome?

As soon as Ricky of the Tuft was old enough to talk, it was clear that everything his fairy godmother had promised had come true. Not only was the young boy clever and witty, he was also very kind and patient. So charming was he that it was easy to forget his ugly face and ridiculous tuft of hair. Everybody who knew Ricky of the Tuft loved him.

Meanwhile, in a neighboring kingdom, two young princesses were growing up. The youngest was, like Ricky of the Tuft, as clever as she was plain, whereas the eldest princess was beautiful, but uncommonly stupid and clumsy. She had so little to say for herself that she found people soon got bored with her and gathered around her witty and intelligent sister instead.

One day, after the princess had managed to knock over three vases, two chairs, and one of the servants who was carrying a tea-tray, the queen lost patience with her elder daughter.

"You are so stupid and clumsy," she cried. "Why can't you be like your younger sister?"

The poor princess was deeply hurt, and she ran out of the palace, through the grounds, and out into the forest. She didn't stop until she reached a quiet glade where she sat down on a grassy bank, her eyes streaming with tears. Suddenly, she noticed a figure coming toward her. She was too upset to see him clearly, but she couldn't help noticing that he was very ugly, even though he was wearing the finest of clothes.

"Why should such a beautiful young woman be crying so bitterly?" asked Ricky of the Tuft gently, for this was indeed the ugly young prince.

At first the princess was unable to answer. She was never very good with words. But the stranger was so kind and gentle that she soon found herself talking to him.

"I may be beautiful," she said, "but to be truthful, I would rather be as plain as my sister, or as ugly as you are. . ." Here she stopped, realizing how rude she must sound.

"Go on," said Ricky of the Tuft, not a bit offended.

". . . if only I had some good sense and wit."

"But you have shown good sense already," said Ricky of the Tuft, "by believing you have none."

The princess looked up at him and smiled. He was a very charming and kind young man, despite his ugly appearance.

"I would love to be clever," she said.

"I think I may be able to help you," said Ricky of the Tuft, who had fallen in love with the beautiful princess. "I have been given the power to bestow upon the person I love best as much good sense as they will ever need."

The princess looked at him, her face shining. "Could you really make me clever and sensible?" she asked. "*Would* you?"

"I have one condition," said the young prince. "And that is that you agree to marry me."

The princess looked at him in horror. "*Marry* you?" she said.

"I can see I have taken you unawares," said Ricky of the Tuft, "so I will give you a year to get used to the idea. I ask that you return to this wood a year from today, and then we shall be married."

The poor princess so longed for good sense and a witty tongue that she found herself agreeing to Ricky of the Tuft's request, and the moment she said yes, she felt a great change coming over her.

When the princess returned to the palace, everyone was astonished at the transformation. Her conversation was suddenly bright, witty, and elegant. It was not long before the word spread around that the eldest princess was now as clever as she was lovely, and many princes from far and distant lands came to the palace to ask for her hand

in marriage. The princess listened politely to their vows of love, but they all sounded very tedious.

"These princes are all so dull and stupid," she told the king. "The man I marry must have a fine and beautiful mind, as well as handsome looks." Needless to say, with all the excitement of her new popularity, she had completely forgotten about her promise to Ricky of the Tuft!

Then, one day, a prince arrived who was not only powerful and rich, but clever and handsome as well.

"You must choose whom you like, my dear," said the king. "But it does seem as though this young man may be the one for you."

The princess secretly thought so too, but she needed time to think.

That afternoon, the princess again went walking in the forest. She had just reached the spot where she had first met Ricky of the Tuft when she was aware of a hustle and a bustle beneath her. She could hear the sound of feet busily running to and fro, and voices calling, "Bring me the cooking pot," and "Put some more wood on the fire."

Suddenly, the ground opened up in front of her. Staring down, the princess saw a huge kitchen, where a splendid banquet was being prepared. Cooks and kitchen-maids hurried back and forth carrying big platters of food, and other servants ran up into the forest to lay out a long table, covered with a snow-white cloth.

"For whom is this magnificent banquet being prepared?" the princess asked a hurrying servant.

"For our master, Ricky of the Tuft, of course," replied the servant. "Tomorrow is his wedding day."

The princess suddenly remembered her promise of a year ago. She wondered whether she could return to the palace quietly and forget all about Ricky of the Tuft, but, before she could move a step farther, the young prince appeared. He was as ugly as ever, but he was dressed in rich and elegant clothes, and his smile was warm and welcoming.

"So you have kept your promise," he said. "Will you now give me your hand?"

The princess blushed and stuttered. "I . . . I haven't yet made up my mind," she said, "but I don't know if I will be able to give you the answer you wish to hear."

"Tell me," said Ricky of the Tuft, "is there anything about me, apart from my ugliness, that displeases you?"

"Oh, no!" cried the princess. "You are the most intelligent, the most charming, and the kindest man that I know."

"Then nothing stands between us but my ugliness," said Ricky of the Tuft. "But if you loved me well enough, you could do something about that."

"Tell me," whispered the princess.

"When I was born," said Ricky of the Tuft, "my fairy godmother not only gave me the gift of intelligence, she also gave the person who truly loved me the power to make me beautiful."

"Then I wish with all my heart that you should be the most handsome prince in the world," cried the princess.

When she raised her eyes to his, she saw before her a dazzlingly handsome prince, the very vision of her heart's desire. And at that moment she pledged herself to Ricky of the Tuft forever.

Some people say that the prince's transformation was not the work of his fairy godmother. They say that the princess had already fallen in love with his kind nature and his charm, despite his ugliness and the ridiculous tuft of hair on his head. She saw only the love that shone in his eyes and the generosity of his smile. Whether this is true, I do not know, but I do know that the two of them were married the very next day and were the happiest couple alive.

THE WONDERFUL FISHHOOK

A Maori tale
retold by Linda Jennings

L ong ago, there lived on an island in the Pacific a woman named Taranga. Now in those far-off days, some of the gods lived upon Earth, and one such chose Taranga to be his wife. In time, Taranga gave birth to four strong sons, but the fifth one, whom she named Maui, was a feeble, weak little fellow. Taranga looked at her little son with great sorrow, for it was the rule of the tribe that only the strong should survive and that the weak and sickly must be killed.

"I will not let you die," said Taranga. "I could not bear it."

So one dark night, she gathered Maui up in her arms and ran with him from the longhouse where she lived with her god-husband and her other children. She found a piece of bone, carved

Maui's name upon it, and hung it around his neck on a piece of woven grass. Then she carried the sleeping baby to the seashore and laid him gently beside her while she made a cradle of seaweed. When she had finished, she kissed Maui gently on the forehead, laid him in the cradle, and pushed him out to sea.

Weeping bitterly, Taranga returned to the longhouse, only to find that her husband had left her. She had broken the law of the tribe by not giving up her baby to be killed, and so the god had left Earth never to return.

The little seaweed cradle drifted along down the coast until it washed up on a lonely shore. Maui opened his eyes and found himself looking up at an old man.

The old man stooped down and read the name that Taranga had scratched on the piece of bone. "Maui," he said and, being wise in the teachings of the gods, he recognized the name as one of the names of power.

"I shall take you home and look after you till you are old enough to return to your family," he said.

Maui soon grew from a sickly baby into a strong and healthy boy. The old man taught him everything he knew and gave him the gift of reading other people's  thoughts. Then, when Maui was twelve years old, the old man sent him out to seek his home.

After many days of wandering, Maui came to the longhouse where he was born. His mother recognized him instantly from the piece of bone that she had once tied around his neck.

"The gods have answered my prayers," she cried. "They have sent you back to me." And she welcomed him into the house. But Maui's four brothers were not so happy. They sensed that there was something special about their youngest brother, and that their mother loved him better than she loved them.

One day, Maui saw his brothers whispering in a corner, and because of his power to understand what was in people's minds, he knew that they were planning to destroy Taranga's love for him.

"We'll get up early tomorrow," they said quietly, so that Maui could not hear, "and we'll take out the canoe and go off fishing without our precious little brother. When we return, we will say that Maui would not get up to come fishing with us, and our mother will see what a lazy, useless boy he is."

That evening, Maui stole away into a hidden corner of the longhouse. He took the piece of bone that had always hung around his neck, and he began to carve a fishhook from it. Then he rolled out his sleeping mat and lay down to rest, his fishhook safely clasped in his hand.

Maui was up very early the next morning, long before his four brothers had woken up. The sun had not yet risen over the sea when he climbed into his brothers' fishing canoe. He lay down on the bottom and pulled some fishing nets over him so that he could not be seen.

Presently he heard his brothers coming toward the boat.

"Maui will still be fast asleep," said one.

"Yes, we'll be far out to sea before he finds out we are gone," laughed another.

"How angry our mother will be at his laziness," said a third.

"He'll no longer be her favorite son," gloated the fourth.

Not until the canoe was far out to sea did Maui sit up and throw the fishing nets aside.

"So, I am still at home sleeping, am I?" he mocked.

"We don't want you here!" cried one of the brothers angrily. "We'll throw you out of the canoe and you'll have to swim home. See how you like that!" And the four brothers started to laugh spitefully.

Maui didn't answer. He simply stared hard at his four brothers, and something in his eyes and in his bearing made them afraid and they fell quiet.

"Now, row," he ordered them. "Row out to sea, farther out than you usually fish."

"But we'll run aground on the reef," protested the youngest of the brothers.

"You'll find the passage through the reef if you look," said Maui in a firm voice. "Go on, row till I tell you to stop."

When they were a long way out to sea, Maui finally ordered them to stop rowing.

"Now, start fishing," he ordered. "I shall lay back and watch you."

All through the long hot day, the four brothers fished, until their throats were parched with thirst and their bodies glistened with sweat. But they dared not disobey Maui. Their little brother had become as fearful as a god.

As the sun sank slowly down below the horizon, Maui told them to rest.

"Now I will fish," he told them, and he took out the bone fishhook he had made.

"What sort of fishhook is that?" asked his eldest brother. "It doesn't even have any bait attached to it."

"Wait and see," said Maui. "I shall catch a fish such as you have never seen before."

He threw the fishhook over the side, and it sank down into the deep water. Then he began to pull. . . and pull. . . and pull. . . Something was coming out of the water, but it was no fish!

The brothers gasped in surprise as a splendid longhouse decorated with pearls and shells rose from the waves.

"It is the house of the son of the sea god," said Maui calmly.

As the house surfaced completely from the water, the brothers saw that it had brought with it a whole mass of land. It was an island — a beautiful, fertile island, with rivers and lakes and green forests, and it was shaped just like a fish.

The brothers were beside themselves with excitement. They leapt onto the island and immediately began to quarrel over who should own it.

The eldest brother claimed the largest portion of the land for his own, but the second brother didn't agree.

"Why should you have the largest piece?" he asked. "I shall fight you for it." Soon all four brothers were fighting. Their clumsy feet made deep valleys, and the rocks they threw at each other piled themselves up into high mountain ranges. So fierce was their fighting that the island broke in two, and the four brothers fell into the sea that lay between the two broken pieces and were drowned.

From out of the glistening longhouse, the sea god's son came out to greet Maui.

"It was foretold that you would bring this island out from the sea," he said. "And now it is yours, to rule as you please."

But Maui thought of the many crowded islands that were scattered around the ocean, and he said, "No, I do not want it for myself. I shall send word to the islanders all around that there is an empty and fertile land where they can settle."

And so the people from Polynesia came to the island in their big canoes, and they settled there for many hundreds of years.

To this day they are known as Maoris, and the beautiful green island is, of course, New Zealand. If you look at it carefully on a map, you will see that it is indeed shaped like a fish that has broken in two.

SAVING THE PENNIES

*A Jewish tale
retold by Adèle Geras*

In my grandmother's bedroom, in the corner opposite the big brown cupboard, there stood an enormous wooden chest. The lid was too heavy for me to lift by myself, and my grandmother often said to me, "Never lift the lid of this chest on your own. If it were to fall on your fingers. . ." She would shake her head then, as though she couldn't bear even to think of it. I was not interested in the contents of the chest. It was full of pillows and sheets and blankets and rolled-up quilts in embroidered white quilt-covers.

"Why do we take all the pillows and blankets and put them away in the chest every morning?" I wanted to know. "It means that we have to make the beds again every night."

"It's not such a terrible thing, to make a bed," said my grandmother. "If we left the beds all ready,

43

the whole apartment would look like a big dormitory. When my children were small and my mother was still alive. . . ah, she was a wonderful woman. Have I ever told you about her?"

"Tell me again."

"We called her the Bobbeh. It means 'Grandmother.' Toward the end of her life she became quite blind, but making the beds at night, every night, was a task that she enjoyed.

It took a long time. . . I had nine living children, remember. The Bobbeh used to take each pillow out of the chest and sniff it carefully. 'This one's Leah's,' she would say. 'This is Matilda's. . . and Sara's and Reuben's,' and so on, sniffing every single one and putting it on the right bed. And she never, never made a mistake."

"Never?"

"Never. She was a remarkable woman."

Sometimes my grandmother wanted to clean the floor behind the chest, and Danny and I would help her pile all the bed linen onto one of the beds and push the chest away from the corner. When it was empty, while my grandmother was busy cleaning the place where it had stood, Danny and I would climb into it and pretend it was a big brown boat that we were sailing across dangerous seas.

"If this chest had wheels," Danny said to my grandmother, "you could push us all over the room. . . all over the apartment. Then it really *would* be like a boat."

"Wheels on a chest!" said my grandmother. "That's all I need. . . a chance to spend my days pushing little children across the floor. . . it's a very good thing that chests are absolutely forbidden to have wheels."

"Forbidden?" I asked. "Who forbade it?"

"The Council of Wise Men in Chelm did."

"Oh, them!" I said. "They're not real. We don't have to listen to them. . . it's not *really* forbidden. Only in a story."

"Have you ever seen a chest with wheels?" asked my grandmother.

"No, never," we said.

"Well, then. It shows that, for once, the Council of Wise Men decided something correctly."

"But why did they?" I wanted to know. "Is there a story?"

"Certainly there's a story. The story of Chaim, the poor teacher, and his wife, Dvora. Take a pillow each to make the sitting a little softer, and I'll tell you."

So Danny and I sat in the chest on two plump pillows, and my grandmother told us the story.

"Many years ago, high up on a hill in Chelm, there lived a poor teacher called Chaim and his wife, Dvora. They were so poor that all they had to eat every day was bread with radishes.

"Occasionally, an onion came their way. Dvora would take a few onion rings and boil them up with water and salt, throw in a couple of chicken feet that the butcher gave away because no one wanted them, and this mixture she would call 'soup.'

" 'The rich,' said Chaim, as he drank the colorless liquid from a spoon, 'have fluffy dumplings to go in their soup, made from matzo meal and chicken fat and egg, flavored with nutmeg and sprinkled with parsley. Their soup is yellow, the color of gold. . . one soup for the rich and one for the poor. . .' and he would sigh and dip his spoon into the bowl.

" 'When was the last time,' Dvora asked, 'that we tasted cake?'

"Chaim thought. 'Six months ago, at the wedding of the rabbi's daughter. Do you remember it?'

"Dvora sighed. 'How could I forget it, a cake like that. Filled with chopped nuts and honey and apples, and sprinkled with cinnamon. Such a cake! A cake to dream about.'

"Chaim pulled thoughtfully on his beard. 'Wife,' he said at last, 'I have a plan. A plan that will result in our very own cake.'

" 'Tell me,' said Dvora. 'A cake is what I would dearly like.'

" 'This is the plan. Do you remember my grandfather's big chest? The one on wheels? Well, we will make a small hole in the lid and lock the chest and give the key to a neighbor to keep. Then, every Friday, just before you light the Sabbath candles, you will put one penny into the chest. And every week, before the Sabbath, I will put a penny in also. We are so poor that the loss of two pennies each week will make no difference to our wealth, but the pennies will add up, and in a year, or maybe even nine months, there will be enough in the chest to make the richest, tastiest cake in the whole history of Chelm.'

"And so it was agreed. The very next Friday, Chaim put his penny into the chest. Before she lit the Sabbath candles, Dvora went to the chest and dropped her penny into it. Both Chaim and Dvora began to have dreams about the kind of cake it would be. . . Perhaps a plum cake? Or one with shavings of chocolate over the top? Thinking about the cake filled their minds every waking moment and for half the night as well.

"By Thursday of the following week, however, Chaim had reached a decision. He was a teacher, and therefore a thinker, and his thoughts had been traveling along this path: 'If Dvora puts a penny in the chest every Friday, there will easily be enough pennies after a year to make a perfectly adequate cake. Why should I waste my penny (which Heaven knows I'm desperately in need of) when Dvora's penny will be quite sufficient? No, I will keep my money and say not a word to Dvora and spend it on something else. . . something I need now.' So Chaim went off to the Synagogue that Friday without putting anything into the chest, and continued putting nothing in it, week after week after week.

"Meanwhile, Dvora (who had the day-to-day cooking to do, don't forget) said to herself, 'I have little enough money to spend as it is. Why should I make myself poorer when Chaim is putting in quite enough money for both of us? After all, what does it matter if the cake is a little smaller, a little less rich? To us, it will still taste like Paradise. No, I will keep my penny and say not a word to Chaim, and try and find a marrow bone for proper soup for once.' So she stopped putting her pennies into the chest.

"Well, the weeks passed and the months passed and when springtime came, Dvora said, 'It's April, Chaim. Nearly a year since we started collecting money for our cake. Let us go and open the chest and count the pennies and plan our wonderful treat.'

"Dvora went to fetch the key from the neighbor and, together, husband and wife approached the chest. Chaim bent to unlock it. As he opened the lid, Dvora started screaming, 'Oh, Chaim, Chaim, we've been robbed! Look! There are only two pennies left. . . Oh, who could have done such a wicked thing?'

"Now Chaim was not clever (because everyone in Chelm is a fool, do you remember?), but he *was* a teacher and therefore could at least put two and two together.

" 'Don't be silly!' he said to Dvora. 'How could anyone have taken our money? Did you not see me with your own eyes unlock the chest, not half a minute ago? No, I accuse you, Wife, of not being honest. I say you have tricked me! You have not been putting in your penny every week, have you?'

"Dvora covered her face with her apron and started crying. '*I* have tricked you? Oh, you monster! How can you accuse me when you are the scoundrel? How? *You* have never put a penny in the chest either. And now we've got nothing. . . No pennies and no cake and almost a whole year gone.'

"She dropped her apron and began to shake her husband until his teeth rattled. He snarled at her and, the long and the short of it was, they both fell into the chest, and the lid slammed down on top of them and snapped tight shut. Well then, Chaim and Dvora began to push and struggle to get out like two kittens in a pillowcase, and the violent movement set the wheels of the chest rolling, and it rolled right out of the house and down the hill into the main street. As you can imagine, the citizens of Chelm had no idea what was happening. There they were, quietly minding their business when, suddenly, along came a huge

contraption, careering toward them, ready to crush them to pulp. And not only that, dreadful screams and shrieks were coming from the inside of the chest, so that half the people of Chelm were convinced that all the devils of Hell were bundled up in there and ran away in one direction, while the other half (composed mainly of children and dogs) chased after the chest, adding their cries to the ones issuing from within its wooden depths. In the end, the chest stopped rolling right in front of the Synagogue. The Chief Sage (yes, wearing his golden shoes on his hands!) came out and quickly sent for a locksmith.

"When the locksmith opened the chest and Chaim and Dvora popped out, all disheveled and with their clothes torn and dusty, everyone stepped back in amazement. The Council of Wise Men listened to what the teacher and his wife had to say, and the Chief Sage invited them both to his house for the evening, because it just so happened that his wife had baked a cake that day.

"Two important laws were passed in Chelm shortly after that. The first was that no teacher should ever live at the top of a hill, and the second law was that, from that day to this, no chest is allowed to have wheels on it.

"Now, jump out of there, both of you, and help me push this boat of yours back into the corner."

TORTOISE TRIUMPHANT

*An African tale
retold by Geraldine Elliot*

"I fail to see," remarked Kamba, the Tortoise, to his wife, "why Njobvu, the Elephant, should give himself such airs – just because he happens to be bigger than anyone else. What does size matter? And Mvu, the Hippopotamus, is almost as bad."

"Ill-mannered and conceited – that's what they are!" Tortoise's wife gave a contemptuous sniff.

"I suppose it is because they are stronger than the rest of us," mused Kamba.

"What if they are? What's the good of strength if you haven't got a brain, I'd like to know?"

"Haven't they got brains?" asked Kamba in surprise. He was a humble character and always thought everyone else was cleverer than himself.

"Not what *I* call brains," replied the Tortoise's wife loftily. "Now, listen to me, Kamba," she

54

continued. "I have got a plan for teaching both Njobvu and Mvu a lesson, and if I am not much mistaken, it won't be long before they will be only too pleased to treat you as an equal!"

"Oh?" Tortoise immediately looked interested. "What is this plan?"

Kamba's wife told him. And, as he listened, Kamba's smile gradually became a grin, and the grin spread and spread until it seemed to go three times around his funny little face.

"Oh, excellent!" he chuckled. "Magnificent! A truly splendid idea! I'll go at once and challenge them." Chortling with delight, Kamba set off to pay a call on Mvu, the Hippopotamus.

Mvu was blowing bubbles in the middle of the river, with only his ears and his little pig-like eyes showing above the water, and Tortoise had to shout at him several times before he paid the slightest attention. At length, he rose slowly to the surface, stared haughtily at Kamba, and told him not to come making a noise on *his* riverbank.

"And since when," demanded Kamba boldly, "has the bank belonged to you?"

"How dare you speak to me like that!" Mvu spluttered with rage. "You miserable little object! You impudent reptile! Go away at once!"

"Why should I, if I don't want to? I suppose you think you are stronger than I am, just because you are a little bigger?"

"Of course, I'm stronger than you!"

"I very much doubt it," said Kamba. "It is all very well to brag like that, but you wouldn't dare to take me on at a tug-of-war!"

"What?" roared the Hippopotamus. "Not take you on? You must be mad! Why, I'd pull you over quicker than a Snake can bite!"

"Not you!" replied the Tortoise. "I'm stronger than I look. Though, mind you, I don't say that *I* could pull you across. . ."

"I should think not!"

"Well, will you take me on at sunrise tomorrow? And if neither of us pulls the other over, we'll pull until the vine rope breaks, and then we shall know that we are equally strong."

56

"I certainly will," said Mvu, the Hippopotamus. "And when I've pulled you across. . ."

" 'Quicker than a Snake can bite,' " murmured Kamba impertinently.

". . .I'll pull you out of your shell and spank you so hard that you'll wish you had never been born."

"So you may think," said Kamba cheerfully, "but we shall see!" And, without more ado, he crawled away to seek out Njobvu, the Elephant.

Njobvu was having forty winks under the shade of a Boabab tree, and he was extremely angry at being woken up by Tortoise. And when Kamba suggested that he was no stronger than himself, the Elephant trumpeted with rage and tore up a tree by its roots, just to show how strong he was.

Putting his head on one side, Kamba looked at the unfortunate sapling.

"Pretty fair!" he said, critically. "Of course, that's only a very young tree!"

"Oh, it is, is it?" bellowed Njobvu furiously. "Well, what about this?" He promptly rooted up another, much larger, tree.

"So-so!" said Tortoise airily. "Not at all bad, in fact. However, I don't suppose you would care to take *me* on at a tug-of-war?"

"Ha, ha, ha!" The Elephant roared with laughter. "That's the best joke I've heard for a long time! You must be mad, Kamba! Why, I'd pull you over quicker that a Bee can sting!"

"Will you take me on at sunrise tomorrow?"

"Certainly I will," replied the Elephant. "And when I've pulled you across. . ."

"'Quicker than a Bee can sting,'" murmured the Tortoise.

". . .I'll toss you up into the air until you are so giddy that you'll wish you'd never heard of a tug-of-war. And then I'll spank you!"

"Well, we shall see," said Kamba coolly. "If neither of us succeeds in pulling the other over, we will pull until the vine rope breaks. Then we will know that we are equally strong. Do you agree?"

"Oh, yes, I agree! But you are going to be sorry for your impertinence. I wouldn't be you for much!"

"And I wouldn't be you for anything!" returned Kamba stoutly, and he crawled away to report to his wife.

That night was spent by Mvu, who was as conscientious as he was conceited, in doing exercises and seeing that his muscles were well oiled. He ate the lightest of dinners, for he believed in going into strict training, even for an affair of this sort. Njobvu, on the other hand,

was quite satisfied that he was by far the strongest animal in the whole countryside and so had just as large a dinner as usual and made no effort to train.

Tortoise spent the night looking for a long, strong vine rope.

At dawn he found it – the longest, strongest rope he had ever seen – and he hurried off as fast as he could to give one end to the Elephant and the other to the Hippopotamus. And because of the length of the rope and height of the grass, neither animal could see the other end and both, of course, thought that Kamba, the Tortoise, was there. But Kamba was somewhere in between, and when he shouted, "Are you ready? Go!" each animal braced himself and pulled on the rope for all he was worth, thinking that with one good tug it would all be over.

To their amazement, they could not make an inch of ground. Again Mvu braced himself, and again and again, and he pulled till his well-oiled muscles bulged. But it made no difference.

"Phew!" he whistled to himself. "The strength of this Tortoise is simply *stu*-pendous!"

Meanwhile Njobvu, the Elephant, was pulling with all *his* might. Never in all his life had he pulled

so hard, but not one fraction of an inch could he gain. And after a while he said to himself, "Phew! The strength of this Tortoise is simply *stu*-pendous!"

Hour after hour passed, and still the Elephant and the Hippopotamus pulled and tugged, and neither would give way, although they both were beginning to tire. At last, Tortoise decided they had had enough so, taking a sharp piece of stone, he carefully cut through the vine-rope, right in the very middle. Instantly there came a terrific splash from one end, and a tremendous crash from the other, for Mvu had been standing on the riverbank and, as the rope gave, he fell backwards into the water. And so great was the splash he made that for the next week he was kept busy replying to the complaints that were lodged by all the Crocodiles and Fish who had been disturbed. Njobvu, in falling, had crashed against a tree, and so great was the impact that the whole tree fell to the ground. It took Elephant quite a while to sort himself out from the tangle of branches, earth and roots, and when he had done so, he found a smiling Tortoise looking up at him.

"I do hope you haven't hurt yourself?" Kamba asked. "That was a fine tug-of-war. I wonder the rope stood up to such a strain! Anyway, I am sure you will agree now that we are equally strong?"

"So it seems!" Njobvu sounded very disgruntled. "I still find it very hard to believe!" He walked away, slowly and painfully, shaking his head in a bewildered kind of way.

Kamba grinned and hurried to the riverbank.

"Are you all right?" he called out anxiously to Mvu. "I must congratulate you on such a magnificent display of strength. We really do seem to be equal, don't we?"

Mvu, the Hippopotamus, was almost too dazed to speak, but he nodded his head in agreement.

"Perhaps you will come to dine with us one evening?" continued Kamba pleasantly. "My wife will be delighted to see you. We might ask Njobvu, the Elephant, to come, too. He is about the only fellow in our class, isn't he?"

Again Mvu nodded and, with an effort, forced himself to speak.

"I am sure we should both be honored," he said, and, closing his little eyes, he sank beneath the surface of the water.

THE PAGODA TREE

A Chinese tale
retold by Linda Jennings

There was once a young man called Tung Yung who lived with his sick father on the edge of a Chinese village. The father had been ill for many years, and poor Tung Yung worked hard in the paddy fields to earn enough money to pay for all the medical care. But in spite of Tung Yung's efforts, they were both very poor, and when finally Tung Yung's father died, there was not enough money left even to pay for his funeral.

Tung Yung was desperate. He could not leave his father unburied, and how was he to make the traditional offerings due to his ancestors?

Now some way from Tung Yung's home there lived a rich merchant who heard of the young man's plight. This merchant was a stingy man, and he quickly saw how he could turn the young man's situation to his own advantage. He sent word to

Tung Yung, saying, "If you come to work for me for three years, I will pay for your father's burial."

Tung Yung knew he had no alternative, so he accepted the merchant's offer, and the merchant duly paid for Tung Yung's father to be buried.

Tung Yung stood at his father's graveside with tears in his eyes, for he knew that he would not be able to return to tend the grave until his three years were up. Then, packing his few belongings, Tung Yung set off over the mountain to the merchant's house.

It was a long walk and the day was hot, so Tung Yung stopped halfway and sat down under the shade of a pagoda tree, weighed down by his own grief and weariness.

"Tung Yung, why do you look so sad?"

Tung Yung looked up, expecting to see a friend or neighbor, but instead he saw a beautiful young girl standing beside him. Encouraged by her kind voice, Tung Yung found himself telling her all about his father's death and the price he had to pay for his father to be buried in the proper fashion. "Three long years," he mourned. "How shall I be able to stand it? I hear the merchant is a hard taskmaster."

The girl touched him gently on his shoulder. "Don't worry, Tung Yung," she said. "I shall come with you, and together we shall share all the work.

In that way, perhaps you will be able to leave earlier than the three years he demands."

Tung Yung hesitated. He was wary of this lovely young girl who seemed to know his name, even though he had never set eyes on her before. And how could he possibly turn up at the merchant's house with a strange girl?

The girl seemed to sense his unease. "Make me your wife," she said. "Then it will be perfectly all right for us to work for the merchant together."

65

Tung Yung didn't know what to do. It was all too sudden, and, besides, he had an idea that this young woman was not all that she appeared to be.

"How can we marry without a matchmaker?" he asked. "It wouldn't be right."

The girl touched the pagoda tree under which Tung Yung had been sitting.

"This is our matchmaker," she said. "Tree, will you let us be man and wife?"

The tree bent down, as if to say yes.

"That's not good enough," said Tung Yung. "The tree is simply bending in the wind. It cannot speak."

"Oh, yes, I can," the pagoda tree suddenly announced in a creaky voice. "And I say that you both must marry."

There was strange magic here, thought Tung Yung, but, whether it was good magic or bad, he could not say. "I must bow to the spirits, though," he said to himself, and so he took the young woman to be his wife.

"I did not say you could bring your wife with you," cried the merchant when Tung Yung and his young bride arrived at the house.

"I will be a great help to you," said the girl. "For I can spin and weave and sew, as well as clean the house."

"Hm," said the merchant. "We shall see about that. I shall only let you stay if you can weave me two dozen pieces of linen within three days."

Tung Yung felt sure his young wife could not fulfill the merchant's demands, but she smiled sweetly at him and said, "Don't worry, my love, it shall be done, you'll see."

During the next three days, Tung Yung saw no sign of his wife weaving the cloth, so he was astounded when, at the appointed time, she went to the merchant and presented him with two dozen perfectly woven pieces of linen.

The mean merchant now saw that the girl Tung Yung had brought with him was someone very special, but he had no intention of telling her so. No, he would find means of getting even more work out of her.

"All right," he said grudgingly, "you can stay, as I promised. But I cannot afford to feed you. If you want that, then you must weave me fifty pieces of fine silk in three days."

Tung Yung was in despair. "How can you possibly weave that amount of silk in three days?" he asked. "Oh, I shall lose you, I know I shall, and I shall have to work on alone for three whole years."

But his wife only smiled and assured him that everything would be all right. Tung Yung was not convinced. He saw no signs of her working at all. She strolled in the gardens and sat in the sun, but did not go near the room where the silk looms were kept.

By the end of the second day, Tung Yung was very worried indeed, for his wife had not produced so much as one piece of silk, let alone fifty. But that night, he woke up to find she was not by his side, so he guessed that she must have started weaving at last.

"I shall just go and see for myself," he said, and he crept to the weaving room and quietly opened the door. He stood in amazement at what he saw. A white crane was dropping a shuttle into his wife's hand, and she in turn threw the shuttle at the loom. Immediately it began to weave the silk, with no help from her at all.

"I must be dreaming," said Tung Yung to himself, as he crept back to bed.

The next morning, Tung Yung's wife went to the merchant and laid fifty pieces of woven silk in front of him.

But still the greedy merchant was not satisfied.

"There is one more task," he said. "If you can embroider this silk in ten days, then I will be able to sell it and purchase some slaves. Then you and your husband will be free to go home. But if you fail," he went on, "then you shall remain with me for a further three years."

The merchant was convinced that he had set an impossible task and felt that he had made a good bargain. For in six years the girl would be able to weave him enough cloth to make him a fortune. But the young woman merely smiled and bowed her head in agreement.

Poor Tung Yung was so worried that he could hardly eat or sleep. He felt sure his wife had promised something that she could not possibly fulfill, and he dreaded the thought of living with the merchant for six years.

On the ninth night, Tung Yung was woken from a fitful sleep by the sound of voices coming from the weaving room.

Once again, he crept toward the door and silently opened it. There at the looms sat his wife and six lovely maidens, all embroidering pieces of silk. Seven cranes were helping them by bringing them thread.

Tung Yung was so astonished at the sight that he fainted clean away.

He awoke to find his wife bending over him. "Don't be afraid," she soothed. "What you saw were my six sisters who came along to help me. Now the embroidered silk is all ready, and we shall be free to leave."

The pieces of silk the girl laid before the merchant the next morning were absolutely magnificent. The silk embroidery glowed with rich colors and intricate designs of birds and dragons. The merchant was quite dumbstruck by the beauty of it. He knew, too, that he could not detain the girl or her husband any longer, and, cursing himself for his stupidity, he let them go.

Tung Yung and his wife began their long walk home over the mountain. On the way, they passed the pagoda tree that had acted as matchmaker, and Tung Yung flung his arms around it. But the tree remained a tree, solid and still.

"I wanted to thank it for giving me such a wonderful wife," he said.

In answer, the girl opened her bag and brought out ten bales of beautiful silk.

"Tung Yung," she said softly, "I must leave you now, for I am not as you see me. I am an immortal, but when I saw that you were in trouble, I took on a human shape and came to help you. Now I must return to the gods, but I will leave you with this parting gift. May it bring you prosperity. Do not worry about anything, Tung Yung, for I will always be watching over you."

Tung Yung stretched out his arms to embrace her, but she rose up into the air and disappeared into the clouds, accompanied by seven cranes.

Tung Yung returned home with a sad heart, but, as his wife had promised, he never had to worry about money again. For when he took the bales of silk to the marketplace to sell them, he made enough money to live comfortably all the rest of his life.

THE WORD
OF POWER

An Iraqi tale
retold by Barbara Sleigh

There was once a Caliph of Baghdad, who was young, rich and wise, but not quite wise enough, for he had made an enemy of the powerful Wizard Kaschnur, and it is not wise to offend those who deal in magic.

One day, the Caliph sat at his ease on a pile of silken cushions, smoking his hubble-bubble and fanned by a beautiful slave, when his thoughts were interrupted by the sound of chatter and laughter outside in the court below. He clapped his hands and sent for his Grand Vizier.

"What is the cause of this clamor?" he demanded.

"It is nothing of any importance, My Lord," said the Vizier, bowing low. "Merely a traveling peddler, who has things to sell the like of which I have never seen before, so beautiful are they."

73

"Then let him be brought before me, so that I too may see them," said the Caliph. And so the peddler was summoned.

He was a squat, ugly, squint-eyed fellow, with a straggling, greasy beard. He bowed so low before the Caliph that his forehead nearly touched the marble floor. But if he was ugly, the things he unpacked from his basket were of surprising beauty. There were necklaces and brooches of pearls and emeralds; there were jeweled rings and bracelets; and daggers with curiously carved handles; and carvings in coral, ivory, and jade.

The Caliph bought several pretty things, and with many respectful bowings, the peddler replaced the rest in his basket. He was just preparing to go when the Caliph said, "Stay! There is something you have left behind. What is that small box on the floor behind you?"

The peddler stooped and picked it up, saying as he did so, "A thousand apologies, My Lord! I have the memory of a squirrel and the impudence of a monkey to leave my trash on Your Honor's marble floor, for that is what it is. Merely something I found lying on

74

the cobblestones of the marketplace."

The Caliph held out his hand for the little box. "It is cleverly made," he said. "And the carving on the lid is curious."

"Then will you not accept it as an unworthy present from a humble peddler? . . . No, no, I will accept no money for it, My Lord," said the peddler. "It is enough that you have shown pleasure in my humble store. There is nothing inside the box but a little powder, and a scrap of parchment with something scribbled on it which I cannot read."

When the peddler was gone, the Caliph opened the box. The powder inside was greenish, with a curious heady smell. Tucked into the lid was a small piece of parchment covered with closely crabbed writing. Neither the Caliph nor the Grand Vizier could make head nor tail of this.

"I am determined to find out what it means," said the Caliph. "Let the most learned men in the land be summoned! Who knows, someone may be found who can read this strange writing."

And so the most learned men in the land came to the palace. They passed the parchment from hand to hand, and wagged their beards over it, and nodded their gray heads, for they all agreed at last that the writing was in Latin.

"What it says is this," said the oldest and most learned of them all, bowing as low as his ancient back would let him. "He who would understand the language of all living creatures, and would transform himself into any fish, fowl, or beast of his choice, must first snuff a pinch of the green powder, while crying out the name of the creature he wishes to become. He must then bow three times to the east, crying in a loud voice as he does so: 'Mutabor! Mutabor! Mutabor!' When he wishes to return to his human form once more, he must bow three times to the *west*, calling out the same word of power: 'Mutabor!' But woe betide him who laughs while wearing the shape of his chosen creature, for he will at once forget the magic word and remain an animal for ever and ever."

After swearing the learned men to secrecy, the Caliph rewarded them well and sent them away. Then, laughing heartily, he said to the Vizier, "By the Beard of the Prophet, it is as well that the peddler

could not read the parchment, for surely the box is beyond price! Tomorrow, at sunrise, let us go out into the country and try our luck with this magic powder."

Next morning, as soon as the sun had risen, the Caliph and the Vizier set out together, leaving their attendants behind. As they walked through the garden, they discussed what kind of animal each of them would choose to become.

"Not a toad, for example," said the Caliph, who had seen one crouching nearby. "Far too ugly!"

"Not a honeybee," said the Grand Vizier, as one buzzed past. "Too hard-working!"

Presently they reached the shores of a lake, on the banks of which a stork was strutting up and down on his long legs.

"Ah! Now, a stork!" said the Caliph. "That is a creature of dignity that I should not scorn to be."

"What can it be saying when it clatters its bill so loudly?" said the Vizier.

"Now is our chance to find out," replied the Caliph. "Luck is with us: there is another bird flying toward it. Let us change ourselves into storks and hear what they have to say to one another. But for the Love of Allah, let us remember not to laugh."

So, at the self-same moment, each of them took a pinch of the green powder and wished to become storks. Then, bowing low three times to the east, they cried, "Mutabor! Mutabor! Mutabor!" And in the twinkling of an eye, storks they were, with long necks, long red beaks, and even longer thin red legs, their black feathers gleaming in the morning sun. They looked at one another in astonishment, but the sound of voices soon drew their attention. The bird they had first seen by the water's edge had been joined by the other.

"You are late, my beloved," said the first stork. "I have waited this long time fearing that something had happened to you. What was it that kept you from your own true love?"

"It was not my wish to keep you waiting, beloved," said the second stork. "But tonight my father has commanded me to dance before a company of guests. So that I do not bring shame upon him, I had to stay and practice what I should do."

"Alas, that I should not be there to see. Will you not show me how you will dance?"

Spellbound, the Caliph and the Grand Vizier watched while, in time with the loud clattering of her bill in a kind of song, the young stork pranced backward and forward on her long legs, hopping and sidling up and down. But when she stood swaying on one red leg while she waved the other high in the air, flapping her white wings and writhing with her long neck, they both burst out laughing, and the two storks flew away.

"That was the funniest thing I've ever seen!" said the Caliph, still shaking with laughter.

But the Grand Vizier stopped laughing suddenly. "My Lord," he said, "we were warned that on no account must we laugh! What was the word of power that would turn you back to Caliph and me to Grand Vizier again? It has quite gone from my mind!"

"It began with M," said the Caliph. "That I do remember. M. . . Mu. . . Mu. . . it is no use. I have quite forgotten what it was." And however many times they bowed to the west, mumbling, "M. . . Mu. . . Mu. . ." they both remained storks. At last they gave it up.

"Allah have mercy on us!" said the Caliph. "For storks we must remain forever."

81

For some weeks, they wandered unhappily along the shore of the lake, living on frogs and small fish, until one day the Caliph said, "I long to hear the sound of human voices again. Let us leave this desolate place and fly over the houses of Baghdad. There we can take refuge on the roof of the palace."

But as they flew over the city, they heard the sound of a great crowd, cheering and shouting: "Hail, mighty Mirza! Lord of Baghdad! Hail! Hail!"

"Now I understand it all," said the Caliph, as they circled overhead. "This enchantment is the work of my enemy, Kaschnur the Wizard, for Mirza is his son. There is no hope for us here." And the two storks flew sorrowfully away.

They flew until their wings grew weary. "I can fly no more," said the Caliph at last. "Night is drawing on. There seems to be a ruin below in which we may shelter for the night."

The ruin showed signs of past splendor. Some of the walls and broken pillars still showed the remains of rich colors. They were about to make themselves as comfortable as they were able for the night, when the Vizier said, "My Lord, this is an evil place!

Do you not hear that sobbing sound, as of someone in torment?"

"Nonsense!" said the Caliph. "It is nothing but the cry of an owl!"

Which is just what it turned out to be. They found her moaning sadly, as owls will, in a small ruined chamber with a broken door. When she saw the two storks, her hooting ceased and she greeted them joyfully.

"Who are you? And what are you doing in this unhappy place?" she asked softly. "Are you too victims of the evil Wizard Kaschnur?"

The Caliph and the Vizier, who of course could now understand owl language, told her their story.

"But what brings you here?" went on the Caliph.

"Like you, I am the victim of that wicked man," the Owl replied. "Kaschnur demanded my hand in marriage for his hateful son, Mirza, and my father, who is King of the Indies, had him thrown from the palace. But by means of a poisoned drink, he turned me into the owl you see me and carried me off to live in this dismal ruin, with nothing but rats and bats to keep me company. As I would not marry Mirza, here I must stay, until someone of his own free will ask me to be his bride."

"Alas!" said the Vizier, "I already have a wife." But the Caliph said nothing, for though the Owl was beautiful − for an owl − who could tell what she would be like as a human?

"I may be able to help you," the Owl went on. "This very night, Kaschnur comes here to feast with his friends in an underground cavern. Often they tell stories of their wicked doings. Perhaps you may hear something that may be useful to you. Follow me."

On silent white wings, the Owl circled the ruined room. Then she led the two storks down a dark

underground passage. Soon, they heard the sounds of shouting and laughter and, peering through a hole in the broken wall, they saw a company of men sitting around a table covered with rich foods and flagons of wine.

"There is Kaschnur himself!" said the Caliph.

"And beside him sits the peddler who gave you the carved box with the green powder!" whispered the Vizier.

"That is his hideous son, who wished to marry me," said the Owl.

There was a sudden burst of laughter from within the hall, and a voice shouted, "Tell us what was this word you gave the Caliph which would turn him back to human form?"

"A Latin word," said Kaschnur. "Of which language he and his Grand Vizier know nothing. The word was 'Mutabor'."

Without a sound, the two storks hurried back up the dark passage on their long legs, and the Owl floated after them on her white wings. When they reached the open air once more, the Caliph turned

and, throwing caution to the winds, cried, "Dear Owl, but for your help we should remain storks to the end of our days. We can never thank you enough. I beg you, will you marry me?"

But before she could reply, both he and the Grand Vizier bowed three times to the west, crying, "Mutabor! Mutabor! Mutabor!" And in the twinkling of an eye, they stood once more in their human form.

And the Owl? She had changed into the most beautiful girl you could wish to see.

And so the Caliph and the Princess and the Grand Vizier returned to Baghdad, where the people rejoiced to see them, for Mirza had already begun to oppress them cruelly.

And Kaschnur and his wicked son? The Caliph sent an army to surround the ruin, and both were taken prisoner while they slept off the effects of their feasting and drinking.

And when both had been compelled to sniff the green powder and turn themselves into rats, they ended their days in the ruined chamber in which they had left the Owl, where they could do no further mischief.

And the Caliph and his bride, and, it is to be hoped, the people of Baghdad all lived happily ever after.

MOOWIS

*An Algonquin tale
retold by Alan Garner*

He was the finest hunter, the greatest fighter, the swiftest runner, of all the tribes of the Algonquin. She was the most beautiful, the most skillful, the boldest maiden.

He could summon chieftains' daughters. She was beloved of warriors.

He wooed her. She mocked him.

She told all who listened of how he had come to her, humble, gentle, naked in his heart. The squaws cackled, and the braves jeered, and he lay in his tent and dared not show his tears. The tears chilled his soul.

It was the time for the tribe to move north for the summer. They broke the winter camp, and the village was bustle and noise, but still he lay in his tent and would not come out, nor would he speak. So they took the tent from over him and left him

87

alone on the prairie, while they went north after the deer and the buffalo.

When there was only the level sky to see him, and the silence to hear him, he moved about among the ashes of the dead fires, and the patches of earth, and the forsaken rubbish, gathering a broken bead, a scrap of rotted leather, a twist of rag, a spoiled headdress; and he took them to a sheltered place among the rocks, where some of the winter's snow still lingered. He gathered the snow, and heaped it, as the village children did, and trimmed it and smoothed it, and rounded a head, and put in stones for eyes and nose and teeth. Then he stuck the bits of trash here and there about the snow, and when he had finished he sang a song.

The tribe watched him come into the camp one cold dawn a week later. He had traveled through the nights to be with them, and by his side was a tall and fierce warrior, a young chieftain of the Cree by the marks on feather and skin. The name of this warrior was Moowis.

She looked on the chieftain and loved him. Her mother offered the hospitality of their tent, but Moowis said that he was on a journey of hardship and that he must sleep out in the open, with no cover from the frosts of spring. So she spent her days in pursuit of a chieftain's love and left him to the stars at night. And she soon came to her desire, for Moowis took her for his bride.

Yet still she could not bring the chieftain to the tent. "When we reach home, my home," said Moowis, "we shall share everything. Until then, be patient," and he gave her a glittering smile.

The Cree lands were farther to the north than the tribe hunted, and Moowis seemed anxious to travel fast, so the new bride and groom took their leave, and her old love, the spurned one, was the last and gayest in the parting.

Moowis urged the way north and would not allow for her softer strength, and he kept to shadows by day, and made most speed by night. She went with him on bleeding feet, uncomplaining at the hurt, as a chieftain's wife should. She endured the edges of the rocks and the thorns of the woods when they came to the northern mountains. She planned the fine clothes she would wear, and the dressing of her tent, and was happy with Moowis, her lord and her love.

On the last day, the sun rose in a clear sky. The first scents of growing were in the air, and she followed Moowis up a long cliff path, with neither shade nor shelter. The straight back of her husband, which she had never seen bend in all their journey, went before her. His chieftain feathers were proud.

Yet there was something.

His body he pressed to the cliff and, for all his strength, there was less speed to his pace. She could keep with him easily. The doeskin across his shoulders sagged, the sleeves wrinkled, the legs were slack. And in the growing warmth of the sun, dark patches spread like sweat.

"Have you the fever?" she said.

But Moowis did not speak again. He stopped, the headdress fell, and she crouched alone, the chieftain's bride, on the mountain path, over a puddle of melt-water and some rags and feathers drying in the sun.

LAKSHMI AND THE CLEVER WASHERWOMAN

An Indian tale
retold by Madhur Jaffrey

*Lakshmi is the goddess of wealth and good fortune, and
she lives in the sky with the stars. Once a year, on
a moonless night late in the fall, people light up
their homes with oil lamps and candles to please her.
This is Divali, the Festival of Lights.*

Once upon a time, a king and queen lived in a
beautiful palace. The queen was rather
spoiled and vain. Every Divali, she would ask her
husband for the most expensive presents. Each
year, the king gave her whatever she asked,
however difficult it was for him to get it.

One particular year, the queen had asked for a
seven-string necklace of large pearls.

The king sent a thousand divers to the far
corners of the earth searching for those pearls.
Just before Divali, the divers returned. They had,

at great peril to their own lives, found just the right oysters and, from them, pulled out only those rare pearls that were large and perfect.

The grateful king thanked the divers profusely and gave them large sums of money for their labors. He sent the pearls to the royal jeweler to be strung, and on Divali morning he was able to present his wife with the gift she desired.

The queen was jubilant. She put on the necklace and immediately ran to the mirror to admire herself. She turned her head this way and that, convinced that she was, indeed, the most beautiful creature in the whole world.

It was the queen's custom to go to the river every morning to bathe, accompanied by a bevy of handmaidens. On this particular morning, when she got to the river bank, she undressed and, just as she was poised to dive into the water, she remembered that she was still wearing her seven-string necklace of pearls.

So she stopped and took it off, laying it on top of her clothes. "Watch my necklace," she called, as she dived off a rock.

The handmaidens watched the necklace carefully, but something happened which even they were unprepared for. A crow flew down from a nearby tree, picked up the necklace, and flew away with it. The handmaidens screamed and shouted, but it was no use. The crow had flown out of their sight.

When the queen found out what had happened, she cried with frustration and anger. She went back to the palace and, still sobbing, told the king of her misadventure. The king tried to console her, saying that he would get her a prettier necklace, but the queen pouted and said that she would not be happy until her seven-string necklace was found.

So the king summoned his drummers and heralds. He ordered them to go to every town and village in the kingdom, telling the people that a reward would be offered to anyone who found the queen's necklace.

Meanwhile, the crow had flown from the manicured palace grounds to one of the lowliest slum areas. Here he dropped the necklace on the doorstep of a poor washerwoman's hut.

The washerwoman did not live alone. She shared the hut with her constant companion, an old, toothless crone, called Poverty. The two were not particularly fond of each other, but they had been together ever since the washerwoman could remember and had become quite used to each other's ways.

As it happened, the two occupants of the hut were away when the crow flew by. The washerwoman was collecting dirty laundry, and Poverty, as usual, was accompanying her. On their way home, they passed the village market where they stopped to hear the king's drummers and the proclamation about the queen's necklace. Poverty began to cackle, "Oh, the ways of royalty! What will they lose next? Why do they bother us common people with their antics?"

But the washerwoman was thinking other thoughts. She had never owned any jewelry and wondered how she would look in a seven-string necklace.

When they got home and the washerwoman put her bundles down, the first thing she noticed was the pearl necklace lying on her doorstep. She picked it up and was about to put it on when a thought occurred to her.

"I have an errand to run," she told Poverty. "I will be back in a minute."

So saying, she rushed off with the necklace and headed straight for the king's palace.

The guards tried to stop her, but when she told them what she was carrying, they escorted her directly to the king.

The king was very happy to get his wife's necklace back. He praised the washerwoman for her honesty and then, picking up a large purse containing the reward money, he said, "Here, take this for your pains. It should keep you well fed and well clothed for the rest of your days."

To his surprise, the king found himself being refused. The washerwoman seemed to have something else in mind. She said, "I am a poor, humble washerwoman, Your Majesty. I do not want the money which you are so kindly offering me. There is one favor, however, that I hope you will grant me. Today is Divali. I want you to decree that no one, not even you, will light any oil lamps in his home. Today I want all houses to be dark. All except mine. I want mine to be the only lighted house in the entire kingdom."

The king, grateful that he had got off so lightly, agreed. He sent out his drummers and heralds with the decree as he had promised. He ordered his palace servants to take down all the oil lamps and to put them into storage for the following year.

The washerwoman rushed home, buying as

many oil lamps along the way as she could afford. She arranged these carefully outside her hut and waited.

Night fell. The washerwoman lit all her lamps and looked around. The rest of the kingdom to the north, south, east and west, lay in total darkness.

Lakshmi had, of course, left the heavens and was ready to perform her yearly duty of going from house to house, blessing with prosperity all those that were well lit. This year, something was wrong. There were no lights to be seen anywhere. Poor Lakshmi stumbled along in the darkness from one house to another, but nowhere could she see the slightest trace of a welcoming glimmer.

Suddenly she spotted a glow of bright lights far away in the distance. She began running toward it.

It was the middle of the night when a very exhausted Lakshmi got to the washerwoman's hut. She began pounding on the door, crying, "Let me in, let me in!"

This was the moment that the washerwoman had been waiting for. She called out to Lakshmi, saying, "I will let you in only on the condition that you stay with me for seven generations."

Just then, the washerwoman looked behind her and saw Poverty trying to creep out through the back door. She rushed to the door and locked it. Poverty began to shout, "Let me out, let me out! You know there isn't room in this hut for both Lakshmi and me."

So the washerwoman said, "All right, I will let you go, but only on condition that you do not

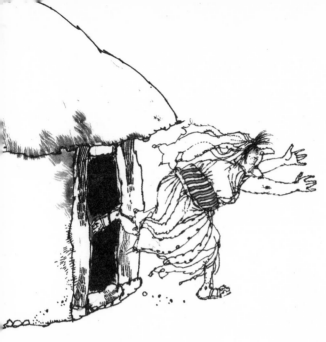

return for seven generations."

Poverty said, "Yes, yes, I will do as you ask. Just let me out of this place. I cannot stand the sight of Lakshmi." At that, the washerwoman opened the back door, and Poverty rushed out.

Then the washerwoman hurried to the front door where Lakshmi was pounding desperately and crying, "Let me in, let me in."

"Only on the condition that you stay with me for seven generations," the washerwoman repeated.

"Yes, yes," said Lakshmi, "I will do anything you ask, only let me in."

And so the poor washerwoman let Lakshmi into her home, and it was blessed with wealth and prosperity for seven generations.

MEDIO POLLITO

A Spanish tale
retold by Linda Jennings

A long time ago, in the Spanish countryside, a fine black hen hatched out a brood of chicks. She was very proud of her little family and clucked and fussed around them, not noticing for a while that the other animals in the farmyard were laughing at her.

"Are my chicks not the most beautiful in Spain?" she said to the pig. But the pig snorted with laughter and replied, "You silly little hen. Can't you see that one of your chicks is only a half-chick?"

When the little black hen looked carefully at her family, she saw that what the pig had said was true. One of her brood looked very strange indeed, for he had only one eye, half a head, half a beak, one wing, and one leg.

"Never mind," said the black hen. "I love you just the same." And she clucked and spread her wings around her little half-chick.

The little chick became known as Medio Pollito, which means "half-chick" in Spanish.

"You must stay at home with me," said his mother. "For your brothers and sisters will grow into fine chickens, but you will be only a half-chick, and everyone outside the farmyard will laugh at you and peck you to pieces."

But Medio Pollito had other ideas. Although he was such an odd-looking little fellow, it didn't stop him from becoming sassy and disobedient.

"Come here!" clucked the black hen to all her chicks. But while all his brothers and sisters ran toward their mother to nestle under her wings, Medio Pollito pretended not to hear her. "I shall explore the farmyard," he said to himself. "Why should I come running every time she calls me?"

Very soon, Medio Pollito became restless. He wanted to find out what lay beyond the farmyard.

"I'm off!" he told his mother one day. "I shan't stay in this boring old farmyard a minute longer!"

And though his mother fussed over him and pleaded with him not to go, Medio Pollito hippity-hopped out of the farmyard and away, without so much as a goodbye.

"I shall go to Madrid to visit the king," he decided, as he hopped along. "I am a very special chick, and no doubt the king will let me live in the palace."

Hippity-hop he went, until he came to a stream that was in a very sorry state, for it was choked up with weeds.

"Help me, Medio Pollito," said the stream. "I cannot flow unless you clear the weeds from the water with your little half-beak."

Medio Pollito looked down his half-beak at the poor stream. "Why should I stop to help you?" he said rudely. "I have more important things to attend to. I am off to Madrid to see the king. No doubt he will give me a very special place in his palace." And he hippity-hopped down the path, leaving the stream to choke with the thick slimy weeds.

Presently, Medio Pollito came to a clearing in the woods. In the middle of the clearing, a wisp of

smoke was rising into the air, and a tiny spark of fire was flickering over some half-burned logs.

"Help me, Medio Pollito," said the fire. "If you can just gather a few more logs to feed me, then I shan't die."

But Medio Pollito just flapped his one wing and said, "Don't bother me with your problems, for I am off to Madrid to see the king. I am sure that he will build me a splendid new chicken coop, all to myself." And he hippity-hopped across the clearing and into the woods, leaving the fire slowly dying under the half-burned logs.

At the edge of the wood, Medio Pollito heard the wind moaning in the branches of a large tree.

"Help me, Medio Pollito," cried the wind. "If you would just untangle me from this tree, then I could fly away."

Medio Pollito stuck his little half-head in the air. "Oh, don't bother me now," he said, "for I am off to Madrid to see the king. No doubt he will build me a fine chicken-run of golden wire." And he hippity-hopped under the tree and away, leaving the poor wind struggling and sighing in the branches of the tree.

Medio Pollito hopped on until at last he came to the city of Madrid with its fine streets and churches. The little half-chick hippity-hopped along the streets to the gates of the palace, and he would have gone straight in had he not met the king's cook on the way.

"Ah, a chicken!" cried the cook and, bending down, she scooped up Medio Pollito and put him in her pocket.

"Just what I need for the stew I am preparing for the king," she said, as she hurried toward the palace kitchens.

"Chop-chop-chop," went her big knife, as she sliced up the vegetables and tossed them into the pot. And when she had stirred them around, she took poor Medio Pollito and tossed him into the pot, too!

"Help!" thought Medio Pollito. "Here I am in the palace itself, but I didn't mean to be part of the king's dinner!"

It was very uncomfortable in the pot. The water swirled around him and splashed over his head.

"Help me, Water!" cried Medio Pollito. "Don't let me drown!"

"Why should I help you?" asked Water. "*You* didn't help me when I asked you to get rid of the weeds from my stream. Drown, then, and good luck to you!"

By now, the cook had lit the fire under the pot, and the water began to bubble and boil.

"Help me, Fire!" cried Medio Pollito. "Stop heating the pot, or I'll boil to death."

"Why should I help you?" asked Fire. "*You* didn't help me when I asked you to feed me with logs. Boil to death, for all I care!"

That might have been the end of Medio Pollito, but at that moment the cook lifted the lid of the pot and peered inside. "Is that the chicken I threw into the pot?" she said. "Why, it's a poor, scraggy-looking thing. There's no meat on it at all. It's quite unfit for the king's dinner."

And she fished Medio Pollito from the boiling water and threw him out of the window.

The half-chick was soaking wet and scalded all over. As he fell from the high window, the wind suddenly whipped him up and swirled him into the air.

"Help me, Wind!" cried Medio Pollito. "Put me down so that I can run off home."

"Why should I?" asked Wind. "*You* didn't help me when I asked you to untangle me from the tree. No, Medio Pollito, I shall throw you high in the air and see where you land."

The wind tossed Medio Pollito up and up, until he landed on a church spire. It swirled him around, from north to south, from east to west, until the little half-chick was quite dizzy.

"There you will stay, Medio Pollito," said Wind. "And I will blow you to and fro, just as I wish. It is your punishment for being so selfish and stupid and vain."

Medio Pollito now has a new name. He is known as Weathervane, and if you look up to the very top of a church steeple, you will see him there, swinging in the wind, round and round, east and west, and north and south.

THE LUCKY TEA-KETTLE

*A Japanese tale
retold by Helen and
William McAlpine*

One morning, in the days when Mount Fuji was worshipped as a god and as the most divine of all nature's children, a young badger, full of gaiety and the warmth of the first sun of spring, gamboled on a remote moorland with abandon. He rolled over and over, turned somersaults, skipped with the long stems of wild bluebells, and squeaked with delight as he dodged the gorse bushes. He stopped at intervals to beat his stomach like a drum with both furry paws – an endearing trick badgers have when they are happy. It makes a jolly "pon-poko-pon-pon" sound, and if there are children nearby, they run to join in the badger's playtime antics.

He was careless of all but his own happiness and, jumping wildly into a clump of tangled grass, he failed to see a straw rope with a noose at the end which dangled from a bamboo stake. The noose slipped down over his shoulders and held him fast. In terror he rushed to escape, but the noose only became tighter, and the more he struggled the tighter it became.

"Oi! Oi!" he screamed out. "Oi! Oi!"

His cries reached the ears of a tinker, who was at that moment trudging home over the moorland. Quickly, he slipped his large bamboo basket from his shoulders and ran to the spot.

"Oya! A poor little badger caught in a trap!" the tinker cried in surprise, and at once he set the creature free.

"Now, Badger Chan, you run home before you are caught in another wicked trap," advised the tinker firmly, but kindly. He stroked the badger's ruffled fur where the noose had bound it and, giving him a few affectionate pats, said again, "Now, be off with you."

The badger was overcome with the tinker's kindness and burst into tears of gratitude.

"How can I ever repay you?" he wept.

"By returning safely to your home at once," replied the tinker and, stroking the little badger again, he started off on his way.

The badger stood for some time watching him go and wondering what he might do to help his rescuer. Suddenly an idea struck him and, calling on his one magic power, he started to transform himself into a beautifully ornamented teakettle. His body grew fatter and rounder, and his fur sleeked into the rich brown luster of an antique kettle. His tail curved into a handle, and his furry paws shrank to become the four feet. Only his pointed and bewhiskered nose projected where the spout should be. Taking advantage of a pause in the tinker's stride as he stopped to adjust the basket on his back, the badger teakettle hopped nimbly into it, and the unsuspecting tinker continued on his way.

"I have returned, Wife," called the tinker when he reached home.

His wife came running and bowed a greeting as he lowered his bamboo basket onto the wooden veranda in front of their small hut. As he removed his straw sandals, she caught sight of the teakettle.

"Ara! Ara! What is this?" she cried, and she and her husband looked at the kettle in astonishment.

They carried it to their room and placed it on the floor, where its dull sheen glowed against the poor threadbare straw matting. They knelt beside it and gazed at it in silent admiration.

"It is indeed a miracle, a miracle," murmured the tinker.

"There is no more beautiful kettle in the whole of Japan," murmured his wife in reply. "Where did you find it?"

"I do not know where it came from," answered the tinker. "Before this moment, I have never set eyes on it."

They fell into silence again, their eyes lost to all but the delicate form of the little kettle.

"It is exquisite enough to give as an offering to the Morin Temple," thought the tinker. And then aloud, "What do you say, Wife, shall we offer it to the Morin Temple?"

"It is too good for us, and I know that the priest will be happy to receive such a treasure," replied his wife.

The tinker picked the kettle up carefully from

the floor, wrapped it in a cloth, and started out for the temple. When the priest saw the kettle, he was greatly surprised, for he could see at once that it was a valuable treasure and wondered how one so poor as the tinker had come by it. He was even more surprised by the tinker's story, and as there was no way of finding out who the owner might be, he readily accepted it for service in the ancient Tea Ceremony at the temple.

When the tinker had departed, the priest examined the kettle more closely and thought to himself, "It is indeed a kettle of exquisite rarity. I shall invite some friends and have a viewing party."

Filled with curiosity as to what the new temple treasure might be, the friends arrived. They sat in a circle on large square cushions on the floor. The paper-screened doors were slid back to their fullest extent, and the room at once became part of the garden with its carefully laid stepping-stones, its large stone lantern and dwarf pine trees. It was a day perfect for treasure viewing.

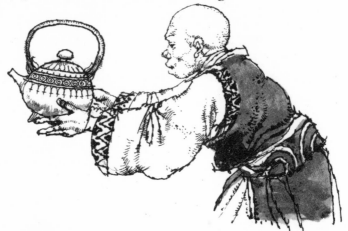

After the first cups of green tea had been served, the priest brought a fine silk cloth and spread it on the floor. On it he placed the kettle, and the guests fell to examining it and praising its simplicity of line, its symmetry, and the luster of the metal. They were exceedingly curious to know where the priest had acquired it, and they listened with rapt attention as he recounted the tinker's story.

"A truly beautiful kettle and worthy of being used for the Tea Ceremony of the temple," said the guests.

"Indeed! Indeed!" answered the priest. "This evening I shall perform the Tea Ceremony and use it. It will add to the purity and refinement of our ritual. Come this evening, my friends, two hours before the sun sets, and we shall partake in a Tea Ceremony party."

That evening, two hours before sunset, the friends gathered in the small outer guest hut in the garden. The priest filled the kettle with water and placed it on the low charcoal brazier. He was about to lay out the Tea Ceremony utensils in their prescribed order, when he heard a loud cry, "Too hot! Too hot!" and to the amazement of everyone there, the kettle rolled off the fire with a bump and a splash to the floor. Out from it sprouted the pointed nose, the fluffy tail, and the furry paws of the badger. He skipped and hopped gingerly around the room, leaving a trail of steam behind him and all the while shouting, "Too hot! Too hot!"

The priest fell back in fear and shrieked, "It is a ghost! It is bewitched!" and fled from the room with his guests close behind him. His young apprentices heard the cries and came rushing in with brooms and dusters to defend him, shouting, "Where is the ghost? What has it done to you, Father?"

Trembling, the priest and his guests put their noses around the door and looked in fear at the kettle, which had now resumed its kettle shape and was reposing innocently in the corner.

Pointing a shaking finger at it, the priest said, "I put that kettle on the fire to heat the water and suddenly it jumped off, crying, "Too hot! Too hot!" and came leaping around the room."

The apprentices chattered among themselves over this miraculous event and gingerly prodded the kettle with their brooms and long-handled dusters. One of them fetched a stone pestle, and with this he prodded the sides of the kettle, saying, "Come, phantom! Show your horns and cloven hoofs!"

But nothing happened, and the kettle remained immobile and innocent as before.

The priest, however, had suffered such a rude shock that he decided to return the kettle to the tinker. Accordingly he sent for him and, after explaining all that had happened, begged the tinker to take the kettle away with him again.

"Well, well, this is certainly a very remarkable kettle," said the tinker, and he wrapped it carefully in the cloth and returned home with it.

That night, after his wife had spread their sleeping mats out on the floor, the tinker placed the kettle at the side of his pillow, and the couple retired to rest. During the night, the tinker was awakened by a voice saying, "Tinker San, Tinker San, wake up!"

Sleepily rubbing his eyes, he saw to his amazement that the kettle had sprouted the sharp, whiskered face, fluffy tail and furry paws of his little badger friend.

"I was so grateful to you for your timely rescue," the little creature said, "that I determined to help you in some way. So I changed myself into a teakettle and hid myself in your basket. I thought you would probably sell me and obtain at least some temporary ease of your poverty. But your nature proved more unselfish even than I had dreamed of, and you and your wife thought only to hand me over to the temple priest. But my interest was in helping you; so I devised a trick to scare the priest into handing me back to you again."

The little bewhiskered kettle chuckled as he continued, "One day, I hope to end my days in the safe shelter of a temple; but meanwhile I assure you there is much we can do together. Now I ask you to open a show-booth, and I will perform for you and make your fortune. I am really quite a skillful fellow, I promise you!"

With this, the badger teakettle fell to performing such amusing dances and acrobatic antics that the tinker was enchanted and saw that there were indeed great possibilities in what the badger said.

The very next day, he set about putting up a show-booth and outside it, on long, streaming banners, he advertised:

> *The Living Teakettle!*
> *The only Live Teakettle that*
> *Dances and Walks the Tightrope!*

The news spread with the swiftness of the wind across the countryside, and large crowds flocked from near and far to gaze at the streaming banners and the bright-colored curtains of the booth. The tinker sat on a high stool at the entrance and called out, "Welcome! Welcome honorable people! Your only chance to see a living teakettle! It dances with the grace of a trembling bamboo leaf! Welcome! Welcome honorable people!"

And he and his wife could hardly keep pace with selling tickets as the people pushed and shoved to gain admittance.

Inside the booth, the air was tense with expectancy. The young girls in their bright-colored kimonos, and young ladies with their hair piled high in rolls glittering with ornaments, twittered like a flock of starlings. Mothers with their babies strapped on their backs chattered ceaselessly to anyone who would listen to them. And the farmers in their conical rice-straw hats gabbled no less than their wives. It was a sea of color and babble, and the only topic of talk was the miracle of the living teakettle.

Kachi-kachi-kachi! The ringing sound of the wooden clappers heralding the start of the show stilled the excited chatter. The audience was tense with anticipation as the curtain rolled back to reveal the tinker kneeling in the center of the small stage. He was dressed in a fine new kimono for the occasion, and bowed low to the audience in

117

greeting. At this moment, the badger teakettle came running onto the stage, and amazement rippled through the audience as he squatted down at the side of the tinker and bowed deeply with the grace and charm of any lady. A whispering like the rustle of dry rice stalks broke out among the spectators: "Look! Look! The teakettle is bowing to us!"

The tinker quietened his delighted patrons with a gesture and, in the loud, dignified voice of a showman, announced, "Honorable people! This rare and wonderful Only Living Teakettle will dance."

With that the badger teakettle opened a small fan and performed an old Japanese children's dance to the delight of the spectators. When the dance was finished, the tinker had to shout through the storm of applause to announce in the biggest voice possible:

"And now, honorable people! The chief attraction of the evening! The world's Only Living Teakettle will walk the tightrope!"

The badger teakettle then bound a cotton scarf around his head as a sign that he was ready to perform an important and dangerous act. The tinker lifted him up onto a rope which stretched high across the stage and handed up to him a paper parasol and a fan. The badger teakettle then performed such spectacular tricks and antics on

119

the tightrope that the crowd yelled with delight and approval and stamped their feet and clapped their hands in tremendous applause.

The teakettle became famous, and every day, folk flocked from town and village, from mountain and moorland, to see him perform; and the tinker and his wife quickly became rich beyond their wildest dreams.

One day, the tinker, who had grown fonder and fonder of his little friend, said, "My dear little colleague! Already you have done far too much for us, and I fear you are becoming tired and overworked on our behalf. I assure you we now have more than we need, and though we shall grieve deeply at parting from you, yet we wish you to return to your own form, whichever it is, and to lead your own life in the way you desire."

He closed the show-booth up from that day and no more shows were ever held. The badger tea-kettle, who in fact really had become very tired, was overjoyed at the success of his plan to help the kind tinker and now wished for nothing better than to end his days in the quiet peacefulness of the temple. So he said farewell with many deep and affectionate bows and salutations to his human friends and returned to his teakettle form. Very carefully, the tinker carried his dear little partner to the Morin Temple, and there he related to the priest in detail all that had happened to him since his last visit. The good priest was full of remorse that he had so much misjudged the badger tea-kettle, but was delighted to hear of the good fortune that had befallen the kind tinker.

"Certainly, this is a rare and valuable tea-kettle," said the priest, "and never again shall I place it on the hot charcoal of the brazier."

He carefully put it in a place of honor in the temple, where it remained for many a long day and may be there still for all I know.

BRO TIGER
GOES DEAD

A Caribbean tale
retold by James Berry

T iger swears he's going to crack up Anancy's bones once and for all.

Tiger goes to bed. Bro Tiger lies down in his bed, all still and stiff, wrapped up in a sheet. Bro Tiger says to himself, "I know that Anancy will come and look at me. The brute will want to make sure I'm dead. That's when I'm going to collar him up. Oh, how I'm going to grab that Anancy and finish him!"

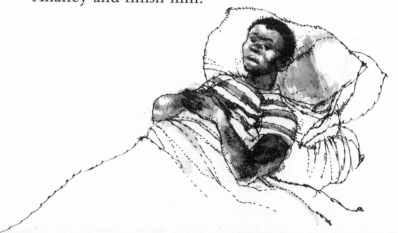

Bro Tiger calls his wife. He tells his wife she should begin to bawl. She should bawl and cry and wail as loud as she can. She should stand in the yard, put her hands on the top of her head, and holler to let everybody know her husband is dead. And Mrs. Tiger does that.

Mrs. Tiger bawls and bawls so loud that people begin to wonder if all her family is dead suddenly and not just her husband.

Village people come and crowd in the yard, quick-quick. Everybody is worried and sad and full of sympathy. The people talk to one another, saying, "Fancy how Bro Tiger is dead, sudden-sudden."

"Yes! Fancy how he's dead sudden-sudden. All dead and gone!"

Anancy also hears the mournful death howling. When Anancy hears it, listen to the Anancy to himself: "Funny how Bro Tiger is dead. Bro Tiger is such a strong and healthy man. Bro Tiger is such a well-fed man. Bro Tiger is dead, and I've heard nothing about his sickness."

Anancy finds himself at Tiger's yard, like the rest of the crowd. Straightaway, Anancy says to his son, "Tacooma, did you happen to hear Bro Tiger had an illness?"

123

Tacooma shakes his head. "No, no. Heard nothing at all."

Anancy goes to Dog. "Bro Dog, did you happen to hear Bro Tiger had an illness?"

Bro Dog shakes his head. "No, no. Heard nothing at all."

Anancy goes to Monkey and Puss and Ram-Goat and Jackass and Patoo and asks the same question. Everyone gives a sad shake of the head and says, "No, no. Heard nothing at all."

The crowd surrounds Anancy. Everybody starts up, saying, "Bro Tiger showed no sign of illness. Death happened so sudden-sudden, Bro Nancy. So sudden-sudden!"

Anancy says, "Did anybody call a doctor?"

The people shake their heads and say, "That would have been no use, Bro Nancy. No use at all."

"Before death came on, did Tiger call the name of the Lord? Did he whimper? Did he cry out?"

"He didn't have time, Bro Nancy. He didn't have the time," everybody says. "It was all so sudden."

Listen to Anancy now, talking at the top of his voice.

"What kind of man is Tiger? Doesn't Tiger know that no good man can meet his Blessed Lord sudden-sudden and not shudder and cry out?"

Tiger hears Anancy. Tiger feels stupid. Tiger feels he has made a silly mistake. Bro Tiger gives the loudest roar he has ever made.

Anancy bursts out laughing. Anancy says, "Friends, did you hear that? Did you hear that? Has anyone ever heard a dead man cry out?"

Nobody answers Anancy. Everybody sees that he is right.

By the time Bro Tiger jumps out of the sheet on the bed to come after Anancy, the Anancy is gone. Bro Nancy is well away.

Nobody even talks to Bro Tiger now. Everybody just leaves Bro Tiger's place without a single word.

THE VISITOR FROM HEAVEN

A Sri Lankan tale
retold by Beulah Candappa

T here was once a rich landlord who was stingy, and, because he was so stingy, he would not sleep at night.

"What?" he shouted, when his wife reminded him that he should go to sleep. "Waste all that time *sleeping* when I could be making more money? Nonsense!" So he stayed awake all night, tossing and turning in his bed, keeping his wife awake, and scheming. . . how to make more money. . .

Every morning, the landlord visited his paddy fields to make sure that his rice plants were flourishing; also to see that no damage had been done by straying cattle or wild animals during the night.

One morning, he discovered his fields in a terrible state. There were bare patches every-where. Many young plants were missing; some had been uprooted and thrown about, while others had been crushed into the mud. Following this trail of destruction, he came across deep, round imprints in the ground, as if something very large and heavy had been driven down into the mud.

"It's the women!" he screamed. "They have been pounding rice in *my* fields!" Fuming with rage, he summoned the villagers.

"Why do you pound your rice in *my* fields?" he demanded. "You have damaged my crops."

The villagers were surprised, and they whispered among themselves, "No one has been in his fields pounding rice. But he is such a greedy man, and greed can make men act foolishly. Maybe that's why he is accusing us. Let's go and inspect the fields."

When they got there and saw the heavy imprints in the mud, they smiled and shook their heads.

"Elephants, Sir! These are elephant footprints. Better keep watch tonight, Sir."

"There are no elephants here. . . tame or wild," the landlord replied angrily. "This is not elephant territory. And *you* know that!"

But the wise old village elders insisted, "These are elephant footprints. There's no doubt about it!"

And so, to prove them wrong, the landlord decided to keep a careful watch that night. He waited patiently in a little thatched hut on the edge of his fields. He was tired and, after some time, he dozed off. Then he woke with a start and peered through the open door. Night had flung its blue-black mantle over the world outside, but one corner of his paddy field was strangely aglow.

"Could it be moonlight?" he asked himself, and then he looked up.

"*Ali-yah*!" ("Elephant!") he gasped in astonishment. A shining, white elephant was slowly floating down from the sky! He could hardly believe his eyes.

"Am I dreaming?" he asked himself, and he rubbed his eyes and looked again.

"No!" he shouted excitedly. "I am not dreaming. There it is!" Gleaming like silver, dazzling in the dark, an extraordinarily large white elephant was nibbling the green and tender paddy plants.

The landlord was completely baffled. "What's the meaning of this?" he exclaimed. "A shining white elephant floating down from the sky. . . from Heaven?"

And then he remembered the stories of the gods his mother had told him when he was a boy.

"Indra, the Hindu king of the gods, rides on a mighty elephant whose skin is as white as snow," she had said. "And that white elephant is supposed to be the very first elephant in the world, and his name is Airavata."

The landlord grew more and more excited.

"The gods must be pleased with me," he said. "Surely this shining white elephant is Airavata. The gods have sent him down to take me to the Garden of Heaven . . . Paradise . . . as a reward for all my goodness. Airavata has been nibbling at my young paddy plants while waiting for me. Those heavy marks in the mud are indeed an elephant's footprints. I must not keep him waiting too long."

Making as little noise as possible, the landlord crept back to his house and told his wife the incredible news.

"Dear Wife," he said, "we have been specially chosen by the gods. The mighty Indra has sent his shining white elephant, Airavata, to take us all to Heaven. Gather all the others together, quickly. This is a great honor for our illustrious family. This is the way to get to Heaven. (And there'll be no funeral expenses for any of our family!)" The old miser chuckled.

The landlord's wife called all her family together – grandparents, sisters, brothers, children, aunts and uncles, cousins, sons-in-law and daughters-in-law. The landlord explained. "Beloved family members," he said, "prepare yourselves for a journey to Heaven."

"Journey to Heaven?" they repeated un-believingly.

"Yes," said the landlord. "We have been honoured by an unexpected visitor. Airavata, god Indra's special white elephant, has floated down from Heaven to visit us. He will be returning the same way shortly. Here is a chance for all of us to go to Heaven together. I will hold onto Airavata's tail, and then we will form a human chain. You, Wife, hold onto my feet; Daughter, you hold onto your mother's feet; Son-in-Law, you hold onto your wife's feet, and so on."

They followed the landlord to the fields. And there, right before them, stood the shining white elephant, Airavata, quietly eating the tender rice plants and making holes everywhere with his heavy feet. The landlord crept up behind and grasped the elephant's silvery tail. His wife held onto her husband's feet, their daughter held onto her mother's feet and, one by one, the whole family clung onto each other.

When Airavata rose majestically into the sky, a long chain of men, women, and children followed him on his journey to Heaven. Up. . . up. . . up. The higher they rose, the more crazily did the human chain swing. . . back and forth. . . as each one clung desperately to the feet of the one above.

The landlord thought he knew all about everything and kept passing messages down.

"It will be so wonderful up there, in Heaven, dear Wife. The trees will be ten times larger than those on earth, the fruit ten times as tasty. . . and the flowers – exquisite!"

The landlord's wife passed every bit of news right down the human chain, but the family were never satisfied. They grew restless and impatient, and as they climbed higher and higher into the

clouds, they asked more and more stupid questions.

The last woman in the chain tugged at her husband's feet and hissed, "Will there be paddy fields in Heaven?"

The answer came back down the line:

"Yes, there will."

She tugged again at her husband's feet.

"Will they be bigger than ours on Earth?"

The answer came back:

"Yes, they will."

One more tug.

"Will they be better than ours on Earth?"

And down the line came the answer:

"Yes, they will."

The next question came immediately:

"Are the rice plants bigger and better, too?"

The landlord was exasperated.

"Of course," he shouted, so that everybody could hear him right down the line. "Their paddy fields are bigger and better. . . and so are their rice plants!"

The last woman in the line sighed contentedly, "Wonderful!" And then everybody sighed happily, right up the line, and the landlord relaxed.

But the landlord's wife was not satisfied.

"If their rice plants are bigger and better than ours, my dear, then their rice grains must be bigger and tastier?"

"Of course they are, my dear," said the landlord, good humoredly.

"Then what about their measuring boxes?" she asked. "Are they, too, bigger and better than ours?"

"Of course they are, my dear," the landlord replied patiently. "Bigger *and* better than ours."

"How big?" shrieked the landlord's wife. Everybody heard her shrieking, and right along the human chain the question came hissing up to the skyline like a smoke signal rising:

"How big? How big? How big?"

"Oh, well!" said the landlord, who knew all the answers. "I wanted it to be a surprise for you. But as you are so impatient, I suppose I shall have to tell you all I know right now."

And then he shouted so loud that everybody could hear him, right down the line, "Their measuring boxes are as big, big, big as. . . *this!*"

He spread his arms out wide to show how large the measuring boxes were in Heaven. And, in so doing, he let go of the elephant's silvery tail. . .

Down. . . down. . . down the whole human chain came tumbling – the stingy landlord, his wife and the rest of their household: grandparents, sisters, brothers, children, aunts and uncles and all. One by one they landed with bumps, thuds, and splashes, back where they started, in the soft, wet mud of their paddy fields.

After that, no one asked any more silly questions.

THE BIRTH OF THE SUN AND THE MOON

An Aztec tale
retold by Linda Jennings

Once the universe was full of darkness. There was no sun, no moon, and no stars, and without their light the world could not grow. All the gods met to discuss what should be done.

"We must appoint a god to become the sun," they said. "Once the warmth of the sun shines upon the world, it will begin to grow and then everything else can be created."

They appointed the god Nanahuatzin for the task. Now, Nanahuatzin was a small and ugly god. His face was scarred with scabs and pimples. He was poor, but he was also gentle and modest.

There was another god in the heavens, called Teccuciztecatl. Teccuciztecatl was as proud and boastful as Nanahuatzin was humble.

"I too shall help create the world," he said in his loud arrogant voice. For Teccuciztecatl could not bear the thought that miserable little Nanahuatzin should receive all the glory.

The creation of the world was a huge and important task. Before they set about it, Nanahuatzin and Teccuciztecatl had to prepare themselves. First they fasted for four days, and then they built a huge fire, into whose fierce flames the two gods had to sacrifice themselves and their riches.

When the time came for the sacrifices, Teccuciztecatl strode forward confidently and threw onto the flames precious stones, gold, and the rainbow feathers from his headdress. Then came Nanahuatzin. The poor little god had no such wealth to sacrifice to the fire. Instead, he offered bundles of reeds, the rags that were his clothes, and even the scabs from his pimples.

But now came the difficult part. Each god had to run through the flames. Again Teccuciztecatl was the first to come forward, but the heat from the blaze terrified him, and he drew back. The fire burned even more fiercely, and the fear of the big, proud god grew even greater. Four times he tried to enter the fire, and four times he drew back.

Then it was Nanahuatzin's turn. He was not a tall god, but he seemed so as he walked calmly and bravely up to the fire and into its searing heat.

Teccuciztecatl felt bitterly ashamed. As Nanahuatzin disappeared into the heart of the blaze, the proud god rushed through after him.

Suddenly the world was bathed in brilliant light, and there, in the heavens, was Nanahuatzin as the sun itself. Very soon afterward Teccuciztecatl appeared as the moon. He too shone with a strong light, as bright as Nanahuatzin's sun.

"This will not do," said the gods, "for it was Nanahuatzin who was brave enough to run through the fire first. It is not right that

139

Teccuciztecatl's light should shine as brightly as Nanahuatzin's."

So they took a rabbit and threw it high up into the heavens in front of the moon to dim Teccuciztecatl's light.

To this day, the moon is less radiant than the sun, and if you look carefully, you will see the shadow of a rabbit lying across it.

BABA YAGA

A Russian tale
retold by Linda Jennings

Long ago, on the edge of a Russian forest, there lived a little girl called Anya. Her mother died when she was very young, and for a little while Anya and her father lived alone. They were perfectly happy together in their small log hut, and so they would have been for many years to come, had not Anya's father married again. Anya's stepmother was a spiteful and cruel woman. She saw at once how much her husband loved his pretty daughter, and she became very jealous of the little girl. From then on, Anya's life was a misery. The stepmother made her do all the hard and unpleasant tasks in the house, and it was "do this" and "do that" from morning till dusk without so much as a "please" or "thank you."

One day the stepmother decided she couldn't bear the sight of her stepdaughter a moment longer. But how could she get rid of her for good? Then she remembered her sister, the terrible witch, Baba Yaga, who lived in the forest, and a wicked plan began to form in her head.

She called Anya to her, and for the first time ever, smiled sweetly at the little girl.

"Anya," she said, "I am making a dress, but my needle has broken. I want you to go into the forest to my sister's house and ask for a new one."

Now Anya knew that the only person who lived in the forest was Baba Yaga, and that anyone who visited her was never seen again, but she was too frightened of her stepmother to disobey. So she set out along the forest path with some bread and cheese tied up in a red polka-dot handkerchief. As she drew near the middle of the forest, Anya began to walk more and more slowly, for she was terribly afraid of Baba Yaga. The old witch was said to have iron teeth with which she ate her victims, and she flew through the air in a mortar and pestle.

All too soon, Anya came to a clearing and there, in the middle, stood Baba Yaga's cottage. It was an odd-looking place. It stood on two chicken's legs and would move itself around so that sometimes it faced east and sometimes west. As Anya came into the clearing, it turned around to face her, and it seemed that its front windows were eyes and its door a mouth. The cottage was surrounded by a fence and, most horrible of all, the fenceposts were topped with the skulls of Baba Yaga's victims.

Trembling, Anya crept up to the gate and opened it. It creaked terribly, as though in pain. Anya noticed a small can of oil by the side of the gatepost, and she oiled the rusty hinges. As she walked up the path, a fierce dog ran up to her, barking and snarling. Anya quickly opened the red polka-dot handkerchief and took out a piece of bread. The poor dog looked half-starved, and when Anya tossed the bread to him, he wolfed it down gratefully and let her pass.

Anya tapped on the door, and it was opened by a thin, untidy-looking girl with hair all over her face. Anya took pity on her, for she looked so miserable.

"Here," said Anya, untying the handkerchief again and putting the cheese in her pocket, "take this handkerchief to tie around your hair."

Suddenly there was a shuffling of feet, and Baba Yaga herself came into the room.

She smiled horribly, showing all her sharp iron teeth.

"And what can I do for you, little girl?" she asked.

"I – I've come to ask for a needle. Your sister sent me," replied Anya.

Baba Yaga's smile grew even wider. She knew how her sister hated her stepdaughter.

"You must be tired and dirty after your long journey," she said. "My servant here will prepare a bath for you. But while you are waiting, sit here and weave some wool for me."

Anya sat down obediently at the loom and began to weave the wool. A scraggy-looking little cat watched her, its paw reaching out to catch the woolen thread as she wove.

"You look hungry, you poor little thing," said Anya, and she took the piece of cheese from out of her pocket and gave it to the cat, who gobbled it up at once.

Meanwhile, Baba Yaga had shuffled out of the door and said to the servant, "Make the bathwater very hot, for I intend to boil and eat this tasty-looking girl."

When the servant heard this, she knew she must warn Anya. The little girl had been kind to her, and now she wanted to repay her by giving her time to escape.

"Take a long time preparing my bath," said Anya when the servant girl told her what Baba Yaga was planning. "Fetch the water in a strainer."

Anya went back to her weaving, her heart beating. How was she to escape from the terrible witch?

"Are you weaving, little girl?" came the witch's cackling voice through the cottage window.

"Yes, Baba Yaga, I am weaving, just as you told me to," replied Anya.

Baba Yaga seemed satisfied, and Anya heard her getting into her mortar and pestle and launching herself into the air.

"She's gone out," thought the girl. "But who knows for how long?"

The little starved cat was watching her with big wide eyes.

"Little girl," she purred, "you have been kind to me, and now I will give you some good advice. Over on that chair is a towel. You will need this when you escape from Baba Yaga. She will try to stop you, but when she approaches, throw down the towel in front of her. That will delay her. She will try again, and this time, you must throw down the comb from your hair. Only then will you be able to get home safely."

Anya thanked the cat, snatched the towel from the back of the chair, and ran out of the door. Already she could hear the swish, swish of Baba Yaga's mortar and pestle as she flew through the air, back toward the cottage again.

The dog outside opened his mouth to bark, but when he saw the nice little girl who had fed him, he closed it again and let her pass. By now, Anya could hear Baba Yaga landing in the yard. Very, very quietly, she opened the gate and, as she had oiled it earlier, it did not squeak. Then she ran as fast as she could, away from the cottage and into the forest.

Meanwhile, Baba Yaga had dismounted from the mortar. "Are you weaving, little girl?" she called.

"Yes, I am weaving, Baba Yaga, as you told me to," said a little voice.

But just as Baba Yaga was about to go off to see if the bathwater was hot enough to boil her supper, she noticed that the figure at the loom had two black pointed ears.

"Aagh!" cried Baba Yaga in rage. "It isn't my sister's step-daughter at all. It's my cat. How *dare* you let her escape and try to deceive me."

The cat gave her a cold stare.

"The little girl gave me a piece of cheese and spoke to me kindly," she said. "When did *you* ever give me so much as a dead mouse?"

The witch snarled and gnashed her teeth with anger and would have kicked the cat out of the door, but she nimbly sprang onto the sill and ran off into the forest.

Next Baba Yaga took the servant girl by the scruff of the neck. "Why did you take so long to prepare the bath?" she asked. "I would have had my supper long ago, if you'd been quicker boiling the water."

"The little girl gave me a red polka-dot handkerchief to tie around my hair," said the servant girl. "You have never given me so much as a ruble for my labors. Why should I not help her?"

Baba Yaga rushed out of the door and shouted at the dog. "You should have warned me! Why did you not bark? Then I would have known the child had run away."

"Why should I have warned you?" asked the dog. "The child was good enough to feed me. You have never given me so much as a dry bone."

Baba Yaga went down the path and kicked savagely at the gate. "You always creak," she said. "Why didn't you creak when the girl went out?"

"Because she oiled my hinges, which you allowed to get all rusty," said the gate.

Baba Yaga slammed the gate in disgust and, jumping into her mortar, she flew up into the air.

"No one escapes from Baba Yaga," she cried, as she rose higher and higher above the forest, until she could see all the winding paths and everything that was going on beneath her. Presently, she noticed Anya far ahead, running through the trees, looking fearfully over her shoulder as she ran.

"Ha, ha, *there* you are!" cackled Baba Yaga, and she flew down through the trees until she could see the little girl quite clearly just below her.

Anya could see Baba Yaga, too. The witch's terrible gleaming iron teeth were gnashing and grinding, her eyes were burning like live coals, and her mortar was now bumping along the ground, just behind her. Anya remembered the little cat's words and threw the towel she had taken from Baba Yaga's cottage. Immediately a wide river appeared and Baba Yaga was left on the farthest bank, shouting and wailing and screaming in anger.

"I'll get you yet!" she cried, and off she flew, back to her cottage, where she drove her herd of cattle all the way down to the river bank. She had cast a spell to make the cattle very thirsty, and it was not long before they had drunk every drop of water in the river and Baba Yaga was on her way again, flying over the trees, until she spotted Anya running ahead of her once more.

Anya saw Baba Yaga coming up behind her again. "She'll surely catch me this time," she said to herself. But then she remembered the little cat's words and, taking the comb from her hair, she threw it down behind her. Immediately a thick hedge of thorns sprang up across the path.

Baba Yaga was quite unable to push her way through the hedge, although she gnawed at the wood with her strong teeth and hammered the thorn bushes with her pestle. The child had defeated her and, with a screech of rage, Baba Yaga returned home to her chicken-leg cottage.

Anya stopped running at last. Her heart was still beating and she was terribly tired, but she was nearly home.

Her father was waiting for her outside their cottage.

"Where have you been?" he cried. "I have been so worried, for your stepmother said you took a walk in the forest and got lost."

Then Anya told her father what had really happened.

"How foolish I have been," cried Anya's father. "How could I have married a woman like that?"

And the stepmother, who had overheard everything, packed her bags and disappeared off into the forest never to be seen again.

But Anya and her father lived happily for many years in the little log hut on the edge of the forest.

A SACKFUL
OF SPIRITS

*A Cambodian tale
retold by Linda Jennings*

Once, long ago, there was a boy who lived with his uncle in the Far Eastern land of Cambodia. He was a very lucky child, for every night an old servant would tell him wonderful stories to send him to sleep – tales of dragons and giants, of kings and princes, of tigers, and other fierce beasts. The boy was enchanted by the tales, which had been handed down to the old servant by his own father, and by his father's father before that. No one else in the village could tell such imaginative tales, and no one but the boy had ever heard them.

The boy boasted about the wonderful stories and, one day, his friends asked if they, too, could come to hear them.

"Of course not," said the boy. "They are *my* stories. The servant tells them especially to me."

"Then tell us them yourself," said one of his friends. "I'm sure you remember them."

The boy remembered them all right, but he was too lazy and selfish to pass them on to his friends. And as you know, all the best stories must be passed on from generation to generation, or else there is trouble.

Now the spirits of the stories that the servant told the boy had become trapped because the boy wouldn't pass the stories on to his friends. The only place for them was in an old bag that hung in the

boy's bedroom. Here the spirits lurked, getting angrier and angrier, for the bag was already crammed full of spirits, and more were added as each night the servant told another story and the boy refused to pass it on.

The boy grew into a fine young man, and still the old servant told him stories, and still he refused to pass them on. Then one day a marriage was arranged for him with a girl from the next village. She was both rich and beautiful, so it seemed the young man was destined for a long and happy life.

On the day before the wedding, the old servant was passing his young master's room when he heard strange whispering noises. He pushed open the door and listened hard. The voices seemed to be coming from an old bag hanging up in the corner.

"He's getting married tomorrow," said one voice. "He's the luckiest young man alive."

"Why should he be free and happy while we're shut up here in this dusty old bag?" complained another voice.

"We must see to it that he *won't* be happy," said a third. "It's all his fault that we are imprisoned here."

The old servant could scarcely believe his ears. What strange spirits were in that bag, and why should they speak so bitterly?

"I have a plan," said the first voice. "I'll disguise myself as a well. He will be very thirsty during the wedding procession and will stop to drink. Little will he know that the water is poisoned!"

All the spirits in the bag cackled spitefully.

"But what if he doesn't drink at the well?" asked a soft voice.

"I have another plan. I'll turn into a strawberry field, but when he eats a strawberry, he will get the most horrible stomach ache."

The third voice could hardly speak it was laughing so much.

"Ah, I have an even nastier trick to play. A servant will place a sack of dry husks underfoot for the groom to step upon. But _I_ will be in the sack, disguised as a red-hot poker!"

"What if all these things should fail?" hissed a venomous voice from deep within the bag. "My plan is to turn myself into a snake and bite him! That will serve him right for refusing to pass our stories on to others and keeping us trapped in here."

The old man now realized what had happened and wondered how he could save his young master. No one would believe him if he told the truth. He would have to act alone. He lay awake all night, planning, and in the morning he rose early to attend the wedding procession.

"May I lead your horse?" he asked the groom, and though the request was not customary, the old man was given the bridle, and the procession set off. Following the groom on horseback was a splendidly embroidered palanquin, ready for the bride.

"Not so fast," cried the bridegroom, for the day was very hot, and he longed to stop for a drink. But the old servant appeared to be deaf. He walked, very fast, up the hill; and, as he passed the poisoned well, he led the horse quickly past it.

Next the procession passed through a field of strawberries.

"Oh, please stop," groaned the groom. "A strawberry would quench my thirst, and they look so delicious."

Again the old man ignored him, and soon the procession had left the strawberry field well behind them. The boy's uncle was getting angrier and angrier at the stubborn old man's refusal to stop and heed his nephew's requests.

"He's getting above himself," he said. "I'll have a stern word with him when we arrive at the wedding."

The procession halted at the bride's house. At once a servant ran forward to place a sack by the horse so that the groom could dismount. But to everybody's surprise and annoyance, the old servant kicked the sack aside so that the groom stumbled and fell.

"He may be my nephew's favorite servant,"

growled the uncle, "but he will be severely punished for this."

What a feast was awaiting the wedding party when they entered the house! A long table was set with golden dishes that were filled with exotic fruits, and delicious meats and sweetmeats. The young man stood at the head of the table and waited eagerly for his bride. He had already forgotten the unfortunate incidents of the journey and the strange way his servant had behaved. At last, the bride appeared from behind a screen. She took her place beside her husband, and they both drank from the wedding cup. The celebrations had begun!

The old servant, however, could neither eat nor drink. He knew his young master's life was still in danger. He did not laugh or applaud the dancers, or the clowns, or the acrobats. He watched carefully as the celebrations drew to their close, but he could spot no danger at the feast.

Daylight faded, and the last of the guests departed. The young couple went to their bedchamber, happy to be alone at last. But not for long. There was a violent banging at the door and, to the young man's annoyance, his old servant rushed in.

"Keep away from the rug!" he shouted, and he ran to the center of the room, wielding a large stick. He pulled up the rug to reveal a large poisonous snake coiled up and ready to strike. He hit the

snake with his stick until it lay dead.

The old servant then explained to the youth exactly what had been planned for his wedding day. He opened up the sack and showed him the poker hidden among the dried husks. He told him about the strawberries and the poisoned well, and about the spiteful spirits who had planned his downfall.

The faithful servant was then rewarded handsomely for what he had done to save his master. And the young man, ashamed of the selfish way he had behaved, told first his bride and then, later, his children, all the wonderful stories that had been told him by the old servant. So the imprisoned spirits were released at last, and the stories have been told and retold through many generations, right up to the present day.